RANSOM

Shadow of an Empire

~

Book II

~

Trial by Time

By Thérèse Judeana

~

illustrated by Grace Bourget

En Route Books and Media, LLC
Saint Louis, MO

⊛ENROUTE
Make the time

En Route Books and Media, LLC

5705 Rhodes Avenue

St. Louis, MO 63109

Contact us at **contact@enroutebooksandmedia.com**

Cover Credit: Grace Bourget

Copyright 2023 Thérèse Judeana

ISBN-13: 979-8-88870-027-3

Library of Congress Control Number: 2023930334

Acknowledgments

The author would like to thank her friends and acquaintances who made suggestions and gave advice; thanks to Chantal LaFortune for feedback and her enthusiasm in reading it.

Most of all, thanks to Christ the True Ransomer for rescuing us all, in time, eternity, and every day of our lives.

Dedication

O Lord I offer Thee This work through Thy only Son,
in the power of the Holy Spirit,
to the praise of Thy eternal Majesty.
- St. Gertrude the Great

To the Hearts of the Holy Family.
In honor of the Holy Face of Christ and Our Lady of La Salette,
that it might help to dry their tears.
For those searching for the key to freedom from sin and hope in
this vale of tears.
And to my Ransomer and my Daystar.

Book II

Trial by Time

I. *Transmission* 1

II. *Tiger's-Eye* 7

III. *Reverie* 15

IV. *Tested* 23

V. *Omen* 35

VI. *Torment* 45

VII. *Lament* 53

VIII. *Sunrise* 61

IX. *Eldritch* 65

X. *Glitter* 77

XI. *Futile* 89

XII. *Slated* 101

XIII. *Bound* 111

XIV. *Possession* 125

XV. *Glacial* 137

XVI. *Entry* 143

XVII. *Archaic* 151

XVIII. *Orion* 157

XIX. *Contradiction* 179

XX. *Hope* 183

XXI. *Falling* 193

RANSOM

Book II: Trial by Time

~~~

"Do not look back to the past, nor forward to the future.
Claim only the present, for it holds God's Will."

- St. Rose Philippine Duchesne

O my God! Source of all mercy! I acknowledge Your sovereign power.
While recalling the wasted years that are past, I believe that You,
Lord, can in an instant turn this loss to gain. Miserable as I am, yet
I firmly believe that You can do all things. Please restore to me the
time lost, giving me Your grace, both now and in the future, that I
may appear before You in "wedding garments."
Amen.

- St. Teresa of Avila

I

Transmission

Computer lights blinked and the oxygen intake hissed softly in the sealed white chamber where the implant's abilities had been tested. Aiyra sat alone in the center of the room, eyes shut as though in meditation now that the wearying tests were over. But her hands restlessly gripped the arms of the chair. Starships and slaves, vortexes and kings. . .

A hole grew in her heart and her eyes flew open when the intercom crackled. Truitt's voice came over, letting her know that she could leave now. Aiyra lost no time, brushing past him and Elise to get to the bridge. She entered and the door shut behind her. Vidara and Briggs turned to her.

"Aiyra! To what occasion do we owe this unexpected visit?" Vidara asked gaily.

"The Shuttle is returning, but my father and Ms. Anselle are not onboard. They have been taken."

"But how do you – we haven't received any transmissions-" Briggs began, but he was cut off.

"Pell to the bridge! We're on our way, but we've lost the Captain and Samantha. Their life signs are nowhere on either ship."

"We know. Aiyra just told us," Vidara answered.

The bridge went still. Everyone's eyes went to the light that glowed red on the intercom; a light always set by the captain when he left the ship so no one would put through an on-board call. Pell would have to be the captain now. But no one knew the father better than the daughter.

"Aiyra, at least until we reach you, and longer if you wish, take your father's place," Pell said finally, his voice grave. "Our ETA is fifteen minutes."

"No," Aiyra replied, crossing the room. She kicked the floor switch and the light turned green. "We will rendezvous with you in seven minutes. Topping, take us out of the atmosphere and prepare to bring shuttle CX-3 back into the cargo bay." She sat down in her father's chair.

"Of course," Topping replied, scarcely ruffled.

In a moment, the *Lumenara* arced over the midnight desert and shot through the clouded atmosphere. Soon she was gliding towards Stratos. A white moonlit dot approached.

"Open the cargo bay airlock," Aiyra commanded, and watched until the shuttle disappeared beneath them. A signal sounded to let them know that the airlock doors were shut behind the shuttle.

"We need to leave the system," she told them. "Six hundred *c*, Ensign."

She arose as the ship literally flew across the system like a horse being given its head in a race. A faint smiled crossed Aiyra's face as she exited, and laid her hand against the cold walls. She could feel the ship's heart beating with exhilaration and knew that her father's love of the *Lumenara* had passed to her.

"You are one of a kind, *Lumen*," she whispered, and continued down to the plaza, where she met Pell and the away team as they were coming up from the bay.

"The water supply is being transferred," Pell said, matching his stride to hers and turning with her as they rounded the garden wall. "The tanks will be full again within an hour."

"That is good. Thank you for your work, commander," she replied.

She studied the light panels in the elevator as they waited to arrive at their floor. Pell paused and softened. He hadn't expected her to do so well, yet things were clearly painful for her.

"What's our heading, princess?" he asked softly as they stepped out.

"I have not given it yet; I wished to wait for you. For now, we are putting distance between us and the system." She stopped outside Pell's cabin door. "I suggest you change and rest; we will meet in the mess hall when you are ready to discuss our course."

Pell bit back a grin. "Thank you, Aiyra. You're doing a fine job in your father's stead. He would be proud of you. I suggest you get the uniform to go with it."

This brought a smile, but the girl just bid him 'til later. When he saw her again that evening, she was clad in a structured dress of Vestar violet and gold with a Captain's star-dusted belt; she bore herself like she had been born into it. They sat down together at a table in the main cafeteria. Someone brought them green tea and wonton soup: a splurge now that water was available.

"We should call Flynn and tell him what happened. We'll see what his orders are," Pell recommended, dropping a handful of oyster crackers into his soup. He watched them bloom to reveal green wasabi peas.

"No. Not yet," Aiyra replied, swirling her green tea and watching it change shades as it formed a vortex. "He will contact us eventually, but let him wait. I have an idea of where to go, and I don't think I can make him understand why."

"Where then?" Pell inquired. They were interrupted by the arrival of Briggs, Topping, and Vidara.

"Hullo, Princess! Er, I mean, Captain," Topping saluted as he took his seat across from her.

"What, onto dessert already Briggs?" Vidara laughed, putting a comforting arm around Aiyra. The two had bonded the moment they had met. Briggs looked up from his bowl of white chocolate cherry-blossom pudding and shrugged.

"Why not? I've had two breakfasts, two lunches, a tea, and half a dinner already, as of two hours ago." He took a scoop of crackers and stirred it into his pudding.

"You're just enjoying the advent of hydrated food," Vidara teased.

"Uh-oh, wasabi-" Topping said aside.

Briggs choked. "Water, water!"

"-Wrong crackers."

Pell shook his head as Briggs downed a glass of water and saved his pudding from the spice. The first officer passed the bowl of tapioca oysters.

"At least you have not *fully* lost your crackers, Briggs," Aiyra smiled.

He shook his head. "Sometimes I think I have!" he joked.

"Yes, sometimes you do," Vidara remarked.

"What's that mean?"

"Perhaps not eating crackers would be a good idea," Aiyra suggested, playfully moving both bowls out of reach. "And starting with dessert may not have been your best idea."

"I do it all the time," Topping commented. "Dessert is practically my middle name!"

"Yeah, tell us how that happened," Briggs said, tentatively tasting his pudding again.

"Well, my family originated in Africa, an Earth country. My great-great grandmother emigrated to Aurelia, a planet in Sector 3, and worked as an interior designer before she married into the Topping family. And you know how they got their name? They were bakers and were known for the extravagant toppings they put on their cakes, and that's been passed down through the family. I'm an exceptional cake-baker myself."

"I never did get my birthday cake," Aiyra smiled.

"Of course, m'lady," he laughed. "You know what amazes me most? That you can keep our spirits up despite everything that's happened. You know, with losing your father and all."

"But he's not dead," Aiyra replied with a mysterious smile. "He just holds the queen and the ace. And Samantha, I think, knows how to handle kings. . . "

~~~

Aiyra entered the bridge and took her father's seat.

"Our heading, m'lady?" Topping asked.

"Set a course for Alnilam in the third quadrant of the Great Galaxy," she replied, her eyes on the digital map before her.

"Alnilam? That's nearly a six-month trip!" Briggs exclaimed.

"Yes, and by the time we reach our destination, we will have learned how to travel through time."

"How?" Vidara asked blankly. She stared as the diagnostics exam disappeared from in front of her.

"I have my ways," Aiyra said with a strange smile, her eyes locked on the deep midnight of space. Three colored dots appeared and slowly aligned on the map's grid. "My implant," she said, "is tied into the trackers carried by my father and Samantha."

"How is that possible?" Briggs gasped. "The signal might be delayed by years!"

"Time occupies the same space, no matter what age it is. Conditions will differ, and stars and moons may be otherwise aligned, but the signal need not travel far if we are near them."

"That doesn't tell us how to switch centuries," Pell pointed out. "We could use the fields, but we don't know how to reach a time of our choosing."

"All we need is a disruptive energy field," Aiyra said calmly. "I know how to build one."

II

Tiger's-Eye

The engines of the Marauder battlecruiser, elite-class, purred softly as it pursued a course through time. Their destination: Mal'lon, the empiric base of the Marauder and his people. It had been their home for millennia; indeed, they had carved it out of time.

Samantha stared into the flickering light of the reflecting pool. The room in which Medrhos had placed her was a near perfect reconstruction of an Almedran cathedral courtyard – royal and beautiful like a Turkish garden, with faint echoes of crystal caves, airy webbing, bells, and strong mountains.

The cat was curled up amongst the shrubs, worn out from her adventures. Gelert lay beside Samantha, his tail thumping rhythmically with the purring of the ship. His mistress didn't respond when he nosed her hand.

Samantha had slowly sunk into a numb lethargy, in part from the strain of the whole day's episode, Medrhos' presence, her agony over Marc and Aiyra, and the fact that Almedrans were always (sometimes unhelpfully) lulled by the sound of water.

The door slid open and Medrhos entered. He stood and watched her for a few minutes; her back was turned. The glass garden-mirror on the far wall had already told her of his presence, but she waited for him to move.

"Do you always enter this silently?" she asked finally. "You remind me of a tiger stalking its prey."

"Usually. . . I did study Arrenian tigers. And I found that the best way to hunt them for pets is to meet them on their own turf and terms; and for sport, to hunt them as they hunt each other."

He sat down opposite her across the pool and she turned her head to meet his gaze. Neither wavered. Samantha wouldn't back down yet. Medrhos spoke first.

"Is the space enough for you?"

"I appreciate <u>something</u> worth seeing on this trip."

There was a moment's silence as Medrhos studied her face.

"No harm will come to you. I would never hurt you-"

"Oh, then what was it that you did to me back there?"

"-Unless it were necessary."

"Then I don't trust you. You could rationalize anything."

"I could. But I don't." There was another pause. "When you're with me," he said at length, "you will have as much space as you desire. Make it your own, Samantha. No one will disturb you. Except me, on occasion." He arose to go.

"As long as you're here-"

Medrhos paused and glanced back.

"Tell me why you changed, and why you've done what you've done!"

"Why I've changed, Samantha?" he asked with a slow smile. "Change is in the heart of every Marauder – as the seasons and circumstances require. When I first saw you, Samantha, I loved you. . . because you alone were quick to trust, innocent and kind; but you were also headstrong and daring. You had what it took to be a Marauder locked up inside of you; even my grandfather said so."

He shook his head, still smiling, and began to walk the perimeter of the pool as Samantha watched him.

"A Marauder child," he continued, "is left free up to the age of twelve, as his elders watch to see what kind of person he becomes and where he is destined to go. Some might be priests of the cult, warriors, leaders, doctors, teachers, tradesmen, or even kings. You see," he explained, drawing himself proudly to his full height, "our kings are chosen for their qualities and abilities, not by their right of ascendancy."

"I see," Samantha drawled. "But you still haven't answered my question."

"When I came to Almedra, I was preparing for the Great Examination. My parents left me in the hands of my grandfather, who at this point had been training me for over a year. I had everything I needed, and it was easy; but I did *not* have the strength or daring I needed to be a warrior or king. Unlike you, I kept it locked up, afraid to take that place lest the throne be destined for someone better than I. My grandfather treated me mercilessly to bring it out, and that is why I needed you as a friend. You helped me through the worst part of my life. By the time I left, I was more than ready for the Examination."

His eyes glinted and he snapped a golden flower from its stalk and cast it into the water, where it floated like some boy's toy boat at play.

"I passed the test as though the part had been written for me. . . and I trained, Samantha, to be a better Marauder than any king before me. You will hear such tales as might frighten you! But you alone are safe from my wrath."

"Then you never were who I thought you were," Samantha murmured, her eyes on the yellow blossom. She touched it and sent it skimming back over the water. "You showed me one side of you that was decaying like the many civilizations that have been lost in time."

Medrhos circled the pool and crouched in front of her, meeting her wounded eyes.

"Almedra was not of my doing," he said softly. "I loved it as much as you. I could, if I chose, restore it; but I have rebuilt it on Mal'lon, where many of your people now live. We saved those who could not escape themselves, Samantha. No one was lost. They will be happy to see you."

He stepped to a hidden window and commanded it to open.

"Come here and look, Samantha."

She complied out of curiosity. Outside the ship was a swirling tunnel of colors and glimpses of life, flashing as the ship sped on.

"Look," Medrhos guided her gaze. "Do you see them?"

Samantha jumped as she realized the presence of thousands of ghostly figures vaguely recognizable as men and women, old and young, all faint and fleeting.

"Like the ghosts on Maedra!" she whispered involuntarily.

"Ah," he said softly, watching her. "With my blood on your scar, you, too, are now attuned to time. They are dead to us," he said, glancing out again. "Some are not even born yet, nor will be for thousands of years, but they live as far as they are concerned. Your captain is out there somewhere if you'd like to say hello."

Stressed, Samantha threw him a look and dropped her shaking hands on the windowsill as she looked out, wondering what was real.

What did the word even mean? And what was time, that it could be played with and distorted this way? Was life only a simulation, like the virtual reality games she had played with Konstan?

But she clung to the one thing she knew, that this chaotic web, even if it were only the strain in her own mind which clouded it, was held by the hands of One Who alone could unravel it when the time was right. She drew a deep breath, bringing her mind back to the little reality she knew, and prepared to leave that agonizing window.

But her eyes caught on brown eyes, so gentle and – no, now a smile – no – now tears, blood, and sweat – But that face! That face she kept seeing! Medrhos seemed to see it too, and he grew disconcerted as he stared out. And olive trees and walls, torches and beaten iron, lightning and floods, rainbows and light –

She gasped and the next thing she knew, her head was in Medrhos' arms as he picked her up from the floor.

"I can't have you fainting, my queen!" he reprimanded her. "You must be rested by the time we arrive." He shut the window and Samantha sat up.

"Can you also tell me why this is taking so long? If you can open a vortex-" she began. Medrhos laughed.

"Even then, it takes time to travel through it. We have several hours to go. I doubt if your captain has arrived at old Cytha yet, though I'm sure he'll consider it worth the wait," he said sarcastically.

"I suppose," Samantha said wearily, "that is how you suddenly appeared on the *Remnant*, but I don't know then how you managed to appear at the right time."

"Actually, we didn't," Medrhos answered, stretching out on one of the low hanging-garden walls. "We have technology that allows us to disrupt ship scanners so that our own life signs, or ships, are not detected. And I must thank you for turning on the life support system before we returned from the *Delta* where we were hiding; breathing apparatuses can be so stuffy. I shall have to get them redesigned."

"We thought you turned them on."

"No. We should have thought of it. Ever tried moving bodies while wearing clunky face masks? It isn't easy."

Aiyra! That was the only possibility – Samantha's eyes went wide and her gaze was drawn towards the window. Oh, if Aiyra knew that the life support systems hadn't been on, and had aided them by turning them on, did she know what had happened?

Medrhos arose again; he seemed restless ever since the appearance of the Face. He looked down into her eyes, then took her hands.

"I promised to give you space, and you shall have it, for close relationships are not things of kings," he said gravely. "But there is one thing I ask of you, and that is this: do not resist when you are asked to become one of us, for if you refuse, your free will shall be taken from you. That is not a thing I would wish for you, Samantha."

"And how do you think that is possible?" Samantha could not help but laugh. "If you try to coerce me, I will resist you all the more."

"Spoken like a true Marauder," Medrhos replied. "Don't you see that all I have done, from the moment I met you to the fear I instilled in you, has turned you into one of us?"

"I am *nothing* like you!" Samantha said angrily.

"That remains to be seen," was his amused reply. "We have our ways, Samantha, and I do not wish it for you, as I have said. It was done to me the day of my examination, after I passed the test, to ensure that my first week of training would proceed smoothly. Once that week was up, things would be easy, for I had already been trained in how to pass it."

Samantha stared, hardly listening as Medrhos added that it was a perfect replacement for imprisonment and punishment. His will had been taken from him – what if –

"You were released?" she asked abruptly. He stopped.

"Quite fully, I assure you. But may I demonstrate?"

He removed a thin gold band from his pocket, with a strange glass-encased, diamond-shaped crystal.

"It only works when laid against one's skin," he explained, seeing her sudden thought at the fact he had it in his pocket. "It matters not how close it is to me otherwise."

He reached out for her wrist but laughed when she pulled away and backed against the wall. He pocketed the bracelet.

"All the same, fear it. As a foreigner, you will be exempt from that law if you can prove that you may be trusted; don't make me do it to you."

He left her then, with swirling thoughts of bound wills, ghosts, and missing loves.

III

Reverie

Swirling, swirling, swirling haze, echoes, burning skies – a cacophony of sound like droning bees over a thundering waterfall. It melted into birdsong and a laughing voice. Marc opened his eyes and was blinded by the late morning sun. It silhouetted a figure in its halo as she bent over him.

"Talitha!" Marc gasped, staring up into her laughing eyes.

"Wake up, silly!" she said gaily. "Do you not know it is your daughter's birthday?"

Marc grasped her shoulders and peered into her face.

"Talitha!" he breathed again.

He knew he wasn't dreaming, for the warmth of the sun and the touch of his wife's hand were real. All the same, he didn't dare let her go. But ought he to kiss her if she were dead and Samantha alive? But for now, he was married – Talitha's voice shook him from his wide-eyed reverie.

"Marc, are you alright? I think you have been sun dazed. You have been out so long today." She felt his forehead but he kissed her instead of answering.

"Silly!" she laughed when he pulled away. "Did you find something for Aiyra?"

Aiyra's birthday – Marc tried to remember. It was her second birthday! That morning he had collected sunshine roses for her deep in the woodland, the kind that don't fade. He reached into the leather pouch he found at his waist and showed the blossoms to Talitha, who clapped her hands with joy. She always had loved the little things best, Marc thought fondly, as he caught her hand and fingered the wedding ring he had made for her, as was Cythian tradition. Talitha cocked her head and smiled at him, quite willing to stay a bit longer.

"I suppose we should go, or we'll miss her birthday feast," Marc murmured, trying to memorize every inch of that beautiful face.

Talitha agreed, and grabbing his hand, dragged him across the meadow, stirring up golden butterflies as they ran through the tall grass. They tagged each other and made it a race to their home. They tore through the archways and into the garden courtyard with its edge overlooking the valley below.

Marc breathlessly dropped his arms on the balustrade and leaned against it as Talitha laid her head on his shoulder, looking out over her home. Lush gardens, green meadows, and thousands of crisscrossing streams and waterfalls fell before them. The cool breeze made rainbows dance in the foam and spray, and far in the distance they could see the glimmer of the ocean. Marc rested his head on Talitha's.

The only sounds were the birds, the breeze, the bubbling of the flowing fountain behind them, and the faint laughter of those preparing the feast for Aiyra. It wasn't every day a princess had a birthday; but the rest was everyday life on Cytha. Marc trembled and slipped his arms around Talitha. He had to save their world, somehow – but he had a little time left to treasure these moments. He shut his eyes and prayed.

~~~

The sun was just rising when Marc woke up. Half-awake, his eyes followed the soft light as it crept through the room and lit up the doorway. Talitha stood there holding their daughter's hands.

"A'da!"

"Aiyra!" Marc exclaimed, sitting up.

The little girl ran to him, giggling, and struggled to climb onto the bed while her mother laughed. Marc pulled Aiyra into his lap and held her tight. It did seem strange to have his daughter as a child when the current-time Aiyra was sixteen – no, by now nearly seventeen. Marc froze.

He had been gone a year now! But was that only for him or for Samantha and Aiyra as well? How could he have left Samantha in her plight? But he could fix everything – but how much *could* he?

"Marc? Marc!" Talitha gently touched his shoulder, her iridescent eyes wide with concern. Marc started and realized his heart was pounding. Aiyra's head was tilted back against his chest as she stared up at him. It hit him that this was the first day he had a chance to change anything.

"It's her birthday!" he smiled.

Aiyra clapped her hands and shook her curls, knowing her parents were going to do something nice for her.

"I'll have to find you a present," Marc declared, squeezing her. His heart rate returned to normal as he understood that he was working on God's timing.

I'll have to watch and listen for Him to show me what to do, he thought. He tried not to stress over his love for Talitha and Samantha and his fear for both.

"Run along with your mother!" he told Aiyra, thinking grimly of the call he would receive later. But right now, he had to remember what he had given Aiyra. . . .

~~~

"Here you are, my little princess!" Marc hung the glassy, teardrop pendant with its nestling pearl, around his daughter's neck.

"Oh, pretty!" Aiyra flung her arms around him and gave him a kiss in return.

They were having the princess' feast in the sunny, glass-ceilinged dining hall. Everyone was there: Talitha's mother and father, Edyin and Mered, who were at home without crowns and gilded robes; her sisters Tirzah and Tryphena, and her brothers Kenan and Hezron; Aiyra's cousins, and everyone's closest friends. Mered arose and proposed a toast for his little granddaughter.

Aiyra sat calmly listening to the traditional ceremony, her pendant clasped in her hands. But when it came to Marc's turn, a chime echoed in the hall. It was the sound of a call coming through the transceiver. He stopped mid-sentence.

Someone glanced at the signal and said it was from Starbase. Marc stared at the wall, glass still in hand. This was the call that had sent him on a wild goose chase while Cytha fell. Would answering it and saying 'no' make a difference? What if he called out the Marauder's deception? No, it would be too much interference –

"Marc?" Talitha inquired, her hand on his arm.

"It can wait," he said simply. "It's Aiyra's birthday, and besides, I already know what it's about. They certainly know how to pick their timing!" he said lightly, and raising his glass, continued the litanic ceremony.

~~~

Five times Marc lived through that year, trying to understand what his role was. Twice Cytha and his family lived and Marc lost his future, and thrice he failed and it was changed. He stopped worrying about what was happening with Aiyra and Samantha. If he could relive the same year over and over without giving up, like he was playing a video game with 'game over' constantly flashing on the screen, he had a feeling God had stopped time in his real life. What great patience He had. . . .

The Marauders came and Marc was there – Cytha was burning now. The people, never warlike, could not defend themselves against the invaders' weapons. The hulking transport ships were rapidly filling with captives. Marc hid among the ruins and watched in agony.

He saw Talitha being shunted into the ship, Aiyra in her arms and blood on her face. Aiyra was calling for him, sure he would save them. Marc moaned and tried to think of something he hadn't tried. He knew now that he could not save his family or Cytha. What in the galaxy was he there for?

Father, help me! he whispered, thinking of the day he had stood on the bridge at the battle of Maltara and that prayer hadn't failed. He let out his breath and let himself shut out the fire and the screams.

No, he wasn't made to stop Cytha from burning, for it was not in his hands. . . . perhaps all he could do was to not give up, to not hate himself for failing when things were in God's hands, and perhaps the best he could do was to ensure that his family didn't die before their time. And so, he tried again.

~~~

When evening had fallen and the children taken outside to play a game, Marc slipped inside and went to the transceiver system. He dropped his hands on the keys and leaned forward, staring at the 'missed call' memo. What would change now that he hadn't answered it? Would they try again, abort their mission, or simply attack and get him out of the way? Would they hunt him down? Should he return the call: say no, yes, or call them out? His thoughts were interrupted by Talitha.

"Marc, what is bothering you, dear?" She searched his eyes. "The whole year, you have been different. . . ever since Aiyra's last birthday. Something is troubling you."

"Something that I can't tell you," he whispered.

"Then I can guess," she answered, moving to his side. "My love, I am not blind. When I found you in the forest a year ago, you were not the same man I married. You had been through more than should be. And now you fear the call that came through – Marc, you have not had a call from the Fleet in two years. You could not possibly know what this call is about, unless you lived passed this time and into the next, and somehow returned."

Marc just looked at her and wondered whether this, too, was creating a mess for the future. Talitha read his thoughts.

"Marc, there are second chances. If you have come back once, you may be here until whatever time that you have found and accomplished His plan. You may well be given the grace."

"Yes," Marc murmured. "I've been through this year six times now, Talitha. . . I can't tell you what's going to happen. It might not be right for you to know. But it seems that all I can do is fail. . . that God made me to fail because He wants me to try, but not to succeed; His plan is strange but I must learn to accept that somehow it is better than what I can do for you, my love, and for Aiyra. You don't belong to me so much as you do to Him and for that my guardianship of you is only temporary, and He can cross it whenever He likes."

He sighed heavily, wondering if it made any sense to Talitha and whether he should have spoken. Talitha turned away as a smile crossed her face and suddenly the lights went out. Marc jumped and looked around. The only light was that of the moon, and Talitha stood in its shaft.

"Marc, have you not guessed?" she asked gently. She stood and waited.

"I was just beginning to," he whispered. "Talitha?"

"Time is stopped, my love. This year has been a test, one to prove to yourself that you are indeed capable of doing what He asks of you. When you were in the vortex, time was paused. Your mind was turned, so that it was in the state, save for your knowledge of events, that it was at this time. I have been told to restore you, for you have passed the test. When Medrhos banished you from your own life, you had finally realized that you were not to blame for your mistakes, as you have learned again. Do you remember this?"

When he hesitated and nodded, she continued.

"Now you must face the real test. My only guidance is do not save us, Marc, for then you would truly fail. All other failures, save for those that would have been caused by the pride you have long since tamed, will be a victory in letting God work in our lives and the lives of many."

Marc tried to understand. Talitha came to him, bringing the moonlight with her, and laid her hand on his brow.

"Peace, my love!"

Marc stirred, eyes wide as he came to himself.

"Talitha!" He tentatively reached out and drew her close. "I don't have much time. . . but if we are outside of time, I may say all the things I wish I could have!"

Talitha smiled up at him and let him pour out his heart. Tears, fears, love, and regret mingled, yet every word brought healing now that he could speak them. She kissed his brow when he finished.

"I am glad we have this gift, my love! Now, do not fear for our daughter. Samantha, however, will need you. There are a few paths you must take before you may save her, and you must find your way through Medrhos' punishment first. I must go now. . ."

She laid her hand on his heart. "Whatever you do, don't fear."

She smiled, stepped away, and vanished.

IV

Tested

The hatch opened with a hiss. Medrhos and his men stood before it and looked out over the city on the towering plateau. The sides fell away into rough-cut green hills like raw emerald, fading into rocky fields and stony deserts. Far, far in the distance gleamed a faint sapphire sea. The king looked down at the thousands gathered about the ship, waiting. Samantha stood half-hidden by the doorway, anxiously studying the sight. It wasn't the volcano and fire she could have expected, but still –

"May the shadows of Rätha never fall!" Medrhos called out.

Samantha made a mental note to inquire as to what this meant. The king looked a little bored with this formality, but his eyes were flashing. What was up with those eyes? Samantha wondered, half-amused. It was almost the only way to read the man's real emotions.

"Our enemy's prince has been punished! We have no fear now," Medrhos proclaimed.

Clearly, he was referring to Marc, but 'prince' threw her for a loop. Marc had never told her about the 'royal side of things' because he hadn't seen the point.

"But I have also found what you have most longed for – we have a queen!"

He pulled Samantha abruptly to his side, leaving her doubly bewildered as the crowd erupted. It was a volcano she *hadn't* expected.

"Why are they reacting like this?" she gasped, involuntarily grabbing his arm and hastily letting go. Medrhos smiled, drinking in the crowd's delight.

"A king is never truly a king until he has a queen. They know you to be good and fair, strong and daring, and now they know that you are beautiful as well," he added. He took her hand and placed it again on his arm.

"It is morning, as you see, and you must get acquainted with your new home before the initiation ceremony begins this evening."

Samantha's heart went cold. She took a deep breath and knew she'd think of something. For now, she had to meet her 'people.' She went down the ramp with Medrhos.

~~~

The torches were lit in the great hall, throwing shadows on the shivering, bold tapestries and shimmering reflections from the sunken pool onto the walls. Carven vines wound about the massive columns, lost among the dim ceiling with its skylight peering into the sunset clouds painted amber and carmine, scattered with violet stars.

Soldiers and guardians lined the walls, Medrhos' most loyal and secretly brother-like. The king had taken his throne, set against a woven wall of stony thorns and sheets of water, regally and terrifyingly imposing.

Samantha stood alone before him, clad in a dress of raven-emerald with a woven metal belt. She blended with the twilight shades among that blaze of crimson-black. There had been no time to rest between being given her chambers, fitted for her new wardrobe, and prepared for the ceremony. Medrhos didn't take his eyes off her, warning her to heed his previous words. Samantha didn't flinch.

She hadn't found any way of escape. When she thought about it, becoming a Marauder was not the *worst* that could happen. The initiation would change her name, place her under Medrhos' guardianship, and grant her the responsibilities of a future queen once she had been trained. There was no mention of renouncing Christianity or becoming a slave-owner; in fact, if Samantha understood things right, there was a little loophole that she could twist so that her responsibilities were to protect them.

But still, there was that 'proof of loyalty.' What form would it take? It seemed it would decide her fate. There was a minute left – the ceremony would begin as soon as the color was wiped from the sky. She brought her focus back to the moment at hand. Medrhos was smiling as though he had read all her thoughts. The last ray of sunlight vanished. He arose.

"Samantha Mariel Anselle! You stand before us tonight for the ceremony of initiation, which will join you to us. Did you choose to join, were you forced, or were you honored?" Samantha suppressed an annoyed look at this formality. If she answered that she was forced, she would be forced to lose her will.

"I did not choose to join," she replied, choosing not to answer more specifically. Medrhos tried not to roll his eyes and signaled the witnesses to go ahead and record the answer anyway.

"This ceremony," he continued, "will test whether you have what it takes to be a Marauder: whether you are quick to think, quick to act, daring when the time calls for it, and when circumstances make it impossible. Tonight, we test your physical and mental abilities."

He turned to sit down again, but whirled and something flashed, heading towards her as he called out a head's up –

Samantha instantly realized it was a blade, but if she stepped back or ducked, she would fall into the pool behind her. The test seemed to require her to catch it without getting injured or falling. All this in a split-second. She spun out of the way, her fingers just barely catching the hilt, and halted, staring at Medrhos, her new plaything in her hand.

"Thanks for the gift," she said with just a hint of irony. "Now I know just how much you care."

"Think swiftly, Samantha, and don't make a mistake. It could well be your last," he said soberly. "Don't fail me."

"I'm not sure about failing *you*-" Samantha began, and abruptly realized the secondary purpose of all the men present as a dozen leapt out at her, swords in hand. Samantha hastily parried a blow, jumping away from the claustrophobic head of the pool so she wouldn't fall into it. She tripped one but was instantly grabbed by another and pulled back, his sword across her shoulders. Samantha struggled.

She was no match, of course, for their strength, but speed, agility, and maybe just a bit of trickery could be her ally. She sank down as though collapsing from loss of breath, and the man let her drop – she hooked one of her legs around his and jerked, causing him to fall over her into the pool as she rolled out from under him. She leapt to her feet and stood panting as two others rushed her. Standing still, she jumped back at the last moment. The soldiers collided and fell to the ground stunned.

That was four of six. The last two would not fall for any of the tricks she had just pulled. Samantha put her back to the column behind her and felt something sticking into her. Her gaze moved upwards and she saw those carven vines and a lone beam stretching high above the pool, from which a lonely lamp was hung.

Samantha leapt up the column, using her knowledge of mountain-climbing to aid her. She jumped, swung out on the lantern and caught her blade on the hilt of another, jerking it out of the man's hand and throwing it into the water. She then vaulted onto the beam and threw the chain at him, before leaping across to the next column, catching the flying chain once more. In a split second she had unhooked the lantern and thrown it at the last unprepared adversary. He took a tumble and the light bulb smashed.

Samantha turned her eyes to the rest of the silent soldiers and wondered how many more she would have to fight. She was exhausted and her limbs trembled. There had been no rest, nor even anything to eat since that morning (though the latter was her fault, not Medrhos'). Samantha looked down at the king, who was shaking his head at the girl who was perfectly at home on the column like a spider in its web.

"How many more of these goons do I have to fight?" Samantha asked, tossing her hair carelessly over her shoulders as though this were nothing new. "I could do this all night! Maybe. . . ."

Medrhos got up and stood beneath the column.

"I can't have you beating up all my best," he laughed. "Come down, Samantha; you've passed this first test."

He held out his arms to help her down.

"I'd be quite happy to knock <u>you</u> flat as well," the girl said lightly, and landed on her feet beside him. He just hid a smile.

"Go rest. Tomorrow will be the second test."

"You're going to drag it all out for a week? I don't suppose we could do them all now and get it over with?" Samantha sighed. "Oh, and incidentally, your rhymes are bland and you could really use a hand."

Medrhos just shook his head again in amusement and answered her question. "No, I'm afraid not. This way my people will get a chance to know you first."

Samantha shook a loose lock of hair out of her eyes and flung the sword back into Medrhos' hands.

"Thanks for the loan."

The king gave her a mock bow. "Always at your service."

"How thoughtful!" Samantha said dryly.

"As always. Until tomorrow, my dear." He showed her out and the great doors swung shut behind her.

~~~

The next morning was a confusing one. It began with Samantha shooting upright in bed and wildly wondering how in the heavens and where in the universe was she. The sprawling sandstone-walled room, with its sunken levels, lattice dividers, and rippling brook spilling over the terrace and down into the mountain gardens hung below, was completely unfamiliar. Except for two things: the cat, and the marriage of Marauder and Almedran elements. Samantha groaned and slapped her forehead as she remembered everything that had happened.

"Poor Marc!" she murmured. "Where are you? But you said you know what you're doing."

She slipped out of bed and looked out the window, running her fingers distractedly through her hair. The gardens were filled with mist, but the sun was high. She had slept later than usual. Flaxen leaves blew in the autumn breeze, and loosened, dusted the balcony before swirling away.

"Poor Aiyra!" she said then. "Now you don't have anyone, even Konstan. . . ."

Would Truitt and Elise be able to remove the implant? She hoped so. She looked down at her hand and slid the medallion-face from the tracker on her wrist. She had attached the medallion to the bracelet which Marc had given her. . . she gently caressed the pearls and then thought of Talitha. Was that good woman watching over her now, perhaps? Or was she about to be saved by her husband?

Samantha cleared her mind of the distracting thoughts as they threatened to scramble her brain again. The Marauders had probably already noticed the constant transmissions, but knew that it would be difficult, even impossible, for anyone to find Samantha and rescue her. Thus, they had left the bracelet alone.

The engineer sighed and turned away from the window. She would have to face the second test that day and she wasn't looking forward to it. Her body was still entirely sore from the last one. Well, there was no sense in trying to put it off. Medrhos might come by and grab her for the test any minute.

Grabbing a two-toned dress of fractaled fuschia and emerald, she changed into it and slipped out. A handmaid, appointed to be Samantha's guide around the palace, was waiting outside the door. She looked at the digital map on her wrist and then led Samantha through the palace. The girl left her in the courtroom, where Medrhos was overseeing a group of young laborers. It seemed the map-it-watch the handmaid used indicated the king's location.

Samantha ducked and darted through the maze of busy workers until she was behind Medrhos. Gelert sat at his side as though he were the one giving orders, with that silly doggy grin. Samantha snapped her fingers and the dog bounded to her side, bouncing on his hind legs like a kangaroo. He nearly knocked his master over in the process.

"What now?" the king asked crossly.

Samantha crossed her arms. "When's this test?"

"Never mind that, we'll get to it later. Can't you see I'm busy?"

"Well, if I'm a bother to you, try un-kidnapping me."

Medrhos looked annoyed. "Run along, Samantha! Take Gelert and find something to amuse yourself until I call for you." He turned away and took no more notice of her.

The girl shrugged and exited. There was one perfect form of amusement: finding a way to escape and taking it. Or perhaps the passengers of the *Delta* were here. Could she locate them?

She came to the great doors of the palace, heavily guarded. Would they let her through? Taking a deep breath, she buried one hand into Gelert's ruff and stepped forward. The guards eyed her for a moment and then pulled open the doors for her.

Relieved, Samantha nodded her thanks and passed through into a terraced plaza of pale stone overlooking the city. A cool autumn breeze wrapped around her, whipping her hair into her eyes. The city below was surprisingly beautiful and ancient as it fell away below her. It was garlanded with jewel-toned rose vines and gilded with leaves of yellow, orange, and crimson, silvered by fountains and streams, and livened by the children playing in the streets and the women who festooned the alleyways with laundry lines and clean sheets.

Samantha softened. There was a normal side to these Marauders, after all. If only when she opened her eyes everything could be normal, peaceful, friendly! But perhaps that was why she was here. She straightened and studied the city more closely.

There was a massive compound at the city's edge. With its high walls and simple buildings, the contrast was so great that Samantha could only assume it was the slaves' village, called Ancil'huin. She didn't hesitate but set out on a long walk. Perhaps Medrhos would regret her freedom, but it had to be done.

~~~

Samantha came up against a wall. Literally. She had finally arrived at the compound after a cautious exploration of the city. She had been allowed within the outer wall of the compound; a channel ran between it and a wire fence that encircled the village. It reminded her sickeningly of a zoo. She tried to convince the master to let her in, but he said he couldn't.

Frustrated, Samantha prowled the catwalk, looking in at the families there. The ground was bare and dusty stone, the buildings plain and rugged, but there were wells, washing pools, and tough food gardens. No one looked happy, but they did seem to be taken care of. Samantha stopped to watch a few children playing in the water. She wondered, miserably, if Aiyra had seen this compound too; whether these children would be saved or enslaved to the Marauders' thought for the rest of their lives. She continued, rounding the village, and came to an ivy-covered brick wall.

Through the nearby lattice she could see, first on the left, a prison ward, and some distance on her right, the only roadway entrance to the city. It was a steep, slippery clay slope framed by the towering rock walls. Ever the slaves were tortured by the nearness, yet the impossibility of escape. Samantha leaned her head on the wall and knew how they felt.

She shook herself and looked around. She couldn't get a view of the prison, so she ran back down the wall and to the other side. The ground dropped away until she was looking into a holding pen where many men were gathered. They looked sick, and the well was filled with lime-tinged water. It was evident that no one had noticed the situation. Samantha found a guard's intercom nearby and impatiently called the master.

"You need to do something before they die! They're sick!"

"Have you been initiated?"

"No, not yet-"

"Then I'm afraid I can't do anything for you. You haven't received responsibilities or authority yet. It will have to wait until a shift change," he said reluctantly, and hung up.

"Then I guess I can do something for myself," Samantha muttered. She swung up onto the narrow wall. Now level with the prison roof, she could see the water system and traced it back to a large rainwater reservoir. The door was shut, but she could hear a faint grinding noise that told her something was up with the mechanisms. Furthermore, the source of the green-tinted water was from the liquid air coolant (the cells were kept rather chilly).

Samantha jumped from the wall to one of the cylindrical beams that crossed from the wall to the building (probably for electrical purposes) and ran across. She soon had the leaking coolant fixed. Did she break into the service room to get the tools? Probably. Was it a problem? Of course not, she was a Marauder.

Next, she found the drainage controls for the pool and traced the electrical current from the reservoir door down the building to the circuitry and discovered a blown fuse. Marauder tech not being too advanced compared to her skills, she soon was able to reset the mechanisms. Samantha watched as a wave of clean rainwater flooded the well and washed it free of the green tinge. She jumped down into the pen. The men stared at her.

"Why did you do that? You'll be punished for helping us."

"Maybe." She helped an injured man to the well. He stooped over it to drink, then looked up into her face. Those brown eyes were familiar: penetrating and kind, almost enchanting.

"My servants punished me; but you are not like them. Even Medrhos looks for this in you." He straightened and reaching out, touched her face. "Lux et pax, dear one," he whispered.

Just then the gate was thrown open by the master, determined to find out who had accessed the supply room without authorization.

"You!" he said, seeing Samantha. "I told you-"

"Why don't you tell Medrhos to cut off my head?" Samantha asked serenely. The man clammed up. He was gently pushed aside. It was Medrhos himself who stood now in the gateway with a knowing smile.

"My lord-"

Medrhos silenced the master with a gesture. "Let her have her way."

"But-"

"You heard what I said. What my lady says, goes." He turned to Samantha. "You passed the second test. Now there is only one left; but before it you are to demonstrate your abilities. Come home now, Samantha."

He held out his hand and looked so proud of her actions that she took it. She glanced back at the men to promise them they would be treated better. The one she had spoken to was nowhere to be seen.

V

Omen

Marc awoke dizzy, the whirling red vortex still imprinted on his vision. It took a few moments for him to be able to see. He slowly picked himself up from the stony outcropping where he had lain and blankly stared for a few minutes at his surroundings before his brain turned back on, righting itself. He was standing on a high gray cliff that curved around for miles before it formed a jagged crescent moon.

Deep in its embrace was held a bustling city, Xirox, and all around, as far as the eye could see, was a rocky desert. There were glimmers of blue here and there, bright like sapphires, but whether it was water or mineral deposits Marc could not tell.

Upon further inspection, he also noticed that the rocks glittered as though crystallized, and deep holes were bored into the cliffs at certain intervals. *Mines*, Marc thought, and raised his eyes to the opposite side of the cliffs. Where once ruins were, the former palace stood, with pennants flying and ships at bay. Maedra, that is, Aliros, before the slaves' rebellion and the rising of the sea.

Before Talitha's death. So Aiyra had been right about his presence here. And Medrhos must have known just where to send him. Was he tempting Marc to save his wife? Could he possibly know the role she had played and what would happen if she were saved?

Marc's heart twisted as though by a wrench. This would be the worst test of his life. He had to try and live it the way God had already seen it. He needed to enter the city and blend in a little, get his bearings and see where to find Talitha and Aiyra. Aiyra had mentioned he had gotten a ride from a merchant traveling by wagon – that this was also where he obtained less 'futuristic' clothing. He turned and squinted at the path that wove through the desert and down the cliffs.

Within five minutes he was riding in the silent merchant's wagon and donning a desert tunic and deep teal cloak with a golden-tasseled hood. He pulled the hood over his head and looked out from the covered conveyance. They passed garden fields with roughly-clad workers while overseers sat lazily in the shade of fruit trees, busy shops where the owners didn't lift a finger, and eateries where the food was fine but the servers were tossed scraps as though they were deserving dogs. Marc frowned and withdrew again into the shadows of the tent-like covering. They were passing the mines now, on a roundabout route to the palatial residence.

Marc's eyes followed the thinly scattered miners who carried crushing blocks of ore to empty carts to be taken to a refinery somewhere in time. He seized the merchant's arm, forcing him to halt the wagon. The captain leapt out and approached one of the miners, a weary girl in a ragged ensemble of dirty white and beige, her brown hair slipping into her eyes as she struggled to load the ore without dropping it too hard or too far. The cart was too tall for her and her arms were, as usual, breaking. Marc put his hand on the rock and took it from her, laying it carefully inside. The girl looked up with a puzzled frown.

"It is radioactive," she informed him. "You should not touch it or even be near it."

"But you are," Marc replied, face half-hidden by the hood. It was well, or his daughter might have seen the flash of wrath in his eyes. Aiyra shrugged.

"That is my job here. They do not care."

"They should," Marc said tersely. A horn call rang out and Aiyra moved to go.

"You are nice – I do not suppose you buy slaves?" she asked over her shoulder.

"No, dear, I don't," he murmured, heart aching. "But I'll see what I can do for you."

Aiyra nodded and walked back into the shadows of the mine. Marc turned his eyes back to the city. He could see the church that had become a rocky island in his time – the foothills which would one day hold the new town. Marc sighed.

He knew that Talitha worked on the far side in the terraced gardens shadowed by the palace. She was an 'ornament' to those who visited there and saw her among the flowers, but she worked as a healer for the court. It was a job she both loved and loathed. There are bad sides to everything under the sun, Marc thought darkly, knowing he'd have to nearly throttle someone later that day. He shook himself. As the merchant had not stopped for him, he set off on foot.

~~~

The woman brushed a loose lock of hair out of her eyes as she bandaged her patient's blistered hand. He had reached into a 500-degree oven and burned himself just because he could. Or so he said.

No, he hadn't heeded his servants' warnings and had taken a dare from a 'brother' nobleman. That hadn't turned out so well.

She shook her head and then wondered who in their right mind thought that court dresses should be a healer's uniform on a hot day when her work required free movement, not taffeta chains. She finished binding his hand as a man entered the apothecary. He made his way to the court-prescribed tearoom and seated himself in a corner where he could view the rest of the room.

"You may go," Talitha addressed her patient. She arose and replaced the medicines behind the counter. The man got up, flexing his already healing wrist, and followed her. He was tall and broad-shouldered, but his most impressive feature was the unpleasant, arrogant smile that made him look like little more than a fool.

"The pretty one has something amazing in her touch," he said admiringly. He leaned on the counter and grinned at her. "Let's stay a little longer." Talitha frowned.

"I would appreciate it if you would not talk to me in that way." She slammed the cabinet shut.

"Oh, why not? I'm not better yet."

"Because you have a brain," Talitha muttered.

"Maybe it needs repairs too."

She gave up. "Because Daruth would not like it!"

"Oh, Daruth's little girl, huh?" he drawled, amused.

"No, I am married and he knows that."

"Who's the lucky one? It's easy to change. . . Come on, who are you married to?" He trapped her behind the counter until she would answer.

"To me!" Marc shed his cloak and strode over, glaring at the highly confused ignobleman.

"Marc!" Talitha gasped.

"Is the man bothering you, dear?" Marc inquired. His eyes were still trained on the fidgeting man's face.

"Yes-"

"But I-"

"You heard what the lady said. I suggest you get out," Marc stated. The man cautiously moved to the door.

"You're not a slave," he wondered.

"No, I'm not, and neither should my wife and daughter be. Get out!"

The man ran. The few patients present were staring. So was Talitha, with wide eyes and a trembling smile.

"Marc?" she whispered joyfully, hardly daring to breath lest he vanish again. Marc stepped forward and took her hands in his.

"Yes, dear."

"Oh, Marc!"

She wanted to sink into his arms after so many years, but she couldn't because of the three intrigued court members. Talitha glanced at them, then restrained herself and turned to her husband.

"We need to be careful," she warned. "They call me Breciendelle here, for they hate my name and I do not know why. It would be best that you call me so if anyone is near. Depending on what Catre and the others tell him, Daruth may be angry."

"I know. I'm afraid he will be." Marc wanted to take her in his arms and reassure himself, to cure that deep chill inside, to freeze her there and not let her go –

"Marc, Aiyra will be so happy!" Talitha whispered, hastily beginning to clean up. She was relieved when the men ceased to watch her. "But. . . they force her to work in the mines," she trembled. "She is very sick, Marc. Why must they torment her and give me something so easy?!"

"I know," Marc soothed her softly, helping her clean the counter. "Believe me, Talitha, she'll be alright. I saw her only an hour ago."

"You saw her? Did you tell her?" Talitha gasped. "How is she?"

"Ssh. . . " Marc watched as two of the three men exited while the third tried to find the sugar cube he had dropped into his tea. "No, I didn't tell her. I didn't know if I should; I didn't want to scare her. But she's strong. She looked a little sick and very tired, but not too bad I think." Talitha sighed and finished sweeping up the loose herbs on the floor.

"I hope the treatment is working. Daruth only lets me treat her because she is my daughter. I wish she could stay home!"

She was watching the last patient and waiting for him to leave. He finally downed his tea and exited. Talitha flopped down on the cushions, exhausted, and her husband sat beside her. His wife was just as beautiful as ever, but weary and more mature than she should be. If only he could tell her she was safe! He bowed his head and asked again if there was a way.

"I am sorry!" Talitha started awake. She came and hugged her confused husband. "I am always tired now," she apologized. "I wish I could really rest. Oh, Marc!" She rested her head on his shoulder and he cradled her. "Marc, I feel so much better now that you are here." They held each other for a few minutes before Talitha forced herself awake again.

"Aiyra's shift ends around sunset; we will have to pick her up. She can hardly manage the walk without someone to guide her," she explained.

"Then it's good that I'm here," Marc replied. "Talitha, is *your* shift over?" She nodded. "Honey, I know you need to rest. But Daruth could come down here at any moment and I fear he'll hurt you-"

"Whenever something happens, he appears at odd hours, like midnight. He won't be around for a number of hours yet," Talitha reassured him. Her husband glanced at the window, still on edge and dreading every moment as it appeared before him. Talitha saw this and gently hugged his arm.

"We can go out," she said softly. "I will be alright. And I am technically free after my workday is over. Want to eat after we pick up Aiyra?" Marc found himself smiling again and he lifted her to her feet.

"Go change out of your uniform then." He kissed her forehead and watched as she left the room. If only he could bring her home! If only there could still be a way, that Talitha's message had been cryptic, that maybe she was not dead but only lost, that Aiyra's past self was not in great danger–

Marc took a deep breath and suddenly scented roses, but not quite – yet there weren't any in the gardens outside. He found himself at peace again and knew that all he could do was take one moment at a time.

He couldn't risk his daughter's safety. . . and he had to remember his words to Samantha: *Because of you, Samantha, I'm no longer tempted to break God's rules. . . and bring her back.* Samantha needed him - in time, Talitha was already home, and Aiyra was where she belonged in God's time. Talitha and Aiyra would live, even if they died or were chained again. His job was to bring them safely to that great Gate which they would all have to pass through, that they would live and breathe and die in His arms. Marc was only their guardian.

~~~

The couple stood anxiously in the de-con waiting room less than an hour later, watching the exhausted workers pass through a series of sterilization chambers. Talitha tried to look down the long line. She was always afraid that something would happen to Aiyra, that she would grow too ill, be injured in an accident, and be terminated by the mining officials. She tried not to imagine it but she shuddered. Marc put his hands on her shoulders and watched.

A thousand faces must have passed before they glimpsed Aiyra far down the line. She was pale and her eyes were half-shut. Patiently she let the moving walkway draw her through the de-con, holding her arms out whenever the lights flashed. At last it brought her out where the walkway ended, but she was too tired to step off. She stumbled into her mother's arms.

"A'ma," she said dizzily. "You are early."

"I know, so are you," Talitha whispered, feeling her daughter's forehead. "I brought your medicine. You will feel better soon, dear." Marc crouched next to them.

"Let's take her out," he murmured, for they were in the way of the conveyor. He picked up the girl, who looked very confused, not having noticed him till now. He carried her out.

"You," Aiyra said drowsily, recognizing him at last. "You remind me of someone. Did you buy us so we can go home?"

Marc bit his tongue so hard he tasted blood.

"No, dear," Talitha murmured hastily. "But he is here to help us."

Marc set his daughter down on a bench outside. The sun was setting and the stars appearing; thankfully, the cool air began to revive the child. Talitha knelt. She wet a cloth which she held to her daughter's brow, and had Aiyra drink from the vial she had brought.

"It helps to reverse some of the effects of radiation," she said aside. "It is made from pholox and brethil, herbs from the gardens. The one helps with nausea and fever, and the other is a healing agent and catalyst for cell regeneration. If I can treat her, she will be fine."

Aiyra opened her eyes and smiled at her mother. "Are we going home?"

"Not yet, dear." Talitha turned her gaze to her husband, and Aiyra noticed him again. She studied his face, which, despite the replacement of the sun with the moon, was now easier for her to see since the hood did not shield his face. The breeze ran its fingers through her hair but it was the only sound as father and daughter looked at each other.

"A'ma?" Aiyra asked, catching her breath with an almost frightened look, barely turning her head aside. She reached for her mother's hand. Then she bolted straight into Marc's arms. Her cries were wordless but he felt them as he pressed her head to his heart. He choked for a second. After fifteen years of failure, he had finally found them.

"Hey there, baby girl!" he breathed. What could he even say? Maybe he didn't need to. She understood. She'd know. He squeezed her.

"Come on, we've got a date for dinner; you and your mother are in dire need of it." He gathered her into his arms as the clock ticked on. Talitha slipped her hand into his elbow and they entered the town which, for a little while, would be safe for them. But only for a little while.

VI

Torment

Bong-skip, bong, skip. Samantha jumped from stone to stone, from which a golden gong was hung, banging with each footfall. Like the soldiers who trained here, Samantha wasn't distracted by the deafening noise. She had dangled high above a gorge, swung across the forest tree tops, forged a raging river, made an all-terrain run through, over, and across the wild-lands in caves, canyons, and narrow crevasses, and now she balanced on a slender column at the end of the course, a thousand feet up, poised as though in a free-flying dance.

Below her lay a staggered staircase of objects which she could only utilize to aid in her soon-to-be free fall. But it was something she was skilled at. She mentally mapped out her course as the wind whipped around her. She heard Medrhos' voice down below and knew that he wanted her to come down. This wasn't one of her tests, so why was he there?

She shrugged and threw herself off the column, catching herself three hundred feet below on a vertical pole, smooth as a pearl, and sling-shotted herself down onto a pile of moss-covered stones. She slid down, flung from the ledge beneath, and landed on her feet in front of Medrhos. That was her short cut.

"Impressive."

"I'm sure you didn't come here to say *that*," Samantha replied, shaking her hair free from its braid and throwing it back over her shoulders. It was really getting a bit long now.

"No, I didn't. Your final test takes place tonight. And my grandfather will be here." He let that sink in.

A chill stabbed through Samantha's arms and into her back, creeping into her head. She shuddered as she remembered Karthos. His presence had somehow been accompanied by specters and visions of dead hands reaching for her soul. She found Medrhos' hand on her shoulder.

For the moment they were again children frightened together. He was calm, but there was a hint of stress in his eyes that strangely led Samantha to relax again. To meet that cruel, cold, calculating, ruthless and conscienceless man who had torn Medrhos' soul – But what could the old man do to the Marauder King? She knew that Medrhos would really have no trouble handling him even if he was afraid.

"You spared me once," he told her. "I'll do my best to return the favor. But I give no promises. I suggest you go rest. I'll call you when it's time to meet him." Samantha nodded and went her way.

~~~

Three hours of restless stress and pacing between the couch and the bed found Samantha pale but collected again, until she was told to dress like an impoverished Cinderella for the test. No, she couldn't wear even her old uniform. Incoming Marauders didn't have the right to dress even that well until they passed the test. Samantha fumed.

Was she less because she was a free, Christian Almedran and not a slave owner or slavery supporter? The rough bone-white gown with its cord was like a penitential habit. The supposed connection between it, a nun, and slavery irritated her. Was she considered nothing unless she was a Marauder? She shook herself when she realized her anger.

She was making too much of it. Medrhos was right. Somehow, he and his grandfather had influenced her with fear and chains until her very instincts became Marauder-like. How could she join them? But she would fit right in. But no, not now that *he* would be there like an icy bird of prey. If she resisted, she'd be enslaved and useless; if she joined – the look on his face – she shuddered again. She shut her eyes and breathed.

"Ransomer, I'll be a slave one way or another," she murmured. "If I must be one, let me be Yours!" She felt peace creeping in amidst her anxious thoughts. She'd just have to move with Him.

~~~

When midnight struck, the doors to the great hall were cast open and Samantha could enter. Torches blazed and the walls were again lined with silent men. Medrhos stood at the throne, clad in robes of smoke and amber. He turned from speaking to a man shudderingly familiar in a jet and blood-spilled garnet robe. She caught herself from hesitating.

Samantha had an invisible army with her – she'd like to think they'd protect her from all harm, but she knew that wasn't their job. She'd deal with him one way or another. Let him think he was on top – she could be unfazed even if Medrhos fell into wrath and fear.

She flung her hair back and crossed the room, carrying herself like a queen; just as Medrhos and Karthos knew she would. But that didn't bother her. It was the smile on Karthos' face that very nearly unnerved her.

She stopped near them, head still high. She gave only a cool nod when Medrhos languidly reintroduced his grandfather. Karthos said nothing, only smiled eerily and looked at his grandson. There was a strained pause. Medrhos hastily exhaled and turned to Samantha.

"Samantha, you are here for your final test. You will join us – or be rejected. One way or another."

"Death, slavery, marooning, or staring dejectedly at you when you marry someone else, I know," Samantha teased. "I don't particularly care which." Medrhos looked vaguely annoyed and she noticed his fingers nervously tapping the sword at his side.

"Begin!" he called sharply.

One of the guards pulled a black tarp from a jet pedestal. A basin of bronze was set on top, filled with stones and a spire in the center, chest high, with an obsidian bracelet clamped there. Instantly, violet-blue flames blazed from the stones and the bracelet burned.

Medrhos took his throne as Samantha stood again at the head of the pool. Ultimate silence reigned. Clearly the fire had an unsettling effect on everyone but Karthos. No one moved.

"Put your hand in the fire," Medrhos said quietly. His eyes were steadily fastened on her now. Samantha did a double-take, looked at the dancing flames, and gave him a confused look.

"I knew you were partially insane, but seriously, I'm not made of stone."

"You won't get hurt! Put your hand in, Samantha."

Samantha slowly raised her hand towards the flame. She couldn't feel the heat; she cautiously stretched out her hand and slipped it through the flames and the bracelet. Nothing happened. She looked at Medrhos; she looked at Karthos; she looked at the men. They were all watching intently. She finally broke the silence as the fire crackled comfortably in the basin.

"Now what?"

"Nothing. You wait. . . you might be here for hours; or maybe only minutes." The King's brow was creased and Samantha began to feel that she should begin to worry about this test. What could they be waiting for? What could possibly happen, but for the fire to die –

"Ah!" she gasped as the flame blazed up and licked her arm. An icy tingling shot through the bracelet, locking her arm and shooting through her body like burning frost, riveting her as though bound in an invisible grasp. She didn't see Medrhos jump and grasp the arms of his chair until his hands were white, nor the anxious glances of the men, nor that cruel spark in Karthos' eyes. It was as though she was a world removed and there was an even stranger silence in her head as she continued to see, but couldn't see.

Disruptor. . . who are you to join them?

"I . . . am. . . the disruptor," she whispered unknowingly.

Join, be loyal, or enslaved. Who are you?!

"The disruptor!"

An icy vise gripped her and Samantha gained control with a struggle. All she could think was that the column must be possessed. Medrhos stirred but his grandfather stopped him.

Ave Maria. . . it searched her thoughts and she tried to block them.

Gratia plena. . . it was maddened and tried to tear her mind.

Dominus tecum. . . peace and oceans, but she could feel the force killing her and stifling her mind as the moon scars flamed white. Medrhos leapt up.

"Samantha, let go!" he cried. "Stop fighting!" Even Karthos was troubled, for the pillar was flashing between blinding white and amethyst fire, and Samantha was dying.

"Son, be still- no one can free her from there." But he was beginning to look concerned.

Et benedictus – blood mingled with the fire.

"Samantha!" Medrhos nearly screamed as he saw the blood flowing from her arm. His sword was in his hand. The pillar cracked ominously and he threw himself forward.

O Maria! The stone shattered. The fire imploded and threw Samantha a dozen feet in the air. Down she fell and the pool's water closed over her head. Medrhos dove in after her, for the pool was deep and sank into a natural water cavern below. Karthos and the men were crowding around when their King appeared. They drew him out, Samantha on his shoulder.

Medrhos tore off one of his gloves and used it to staunch the unrelenting gush of blood from Samantha's wrist. The girl slowly awakened and shook her hair out of her face. Her body ached. But Karthos – she had to show him.

She forced herself to her feet before him and looked again as a queen. Surely, she hadn't passed the test. The flash of worry had been replaced again by Karthos' icy plotting. Let them put her in chains then! Karthos sized her up and glanced deprecatingly at Medrhos, who threw his head back and grew cold again.

"You need an heir if you want to remain King without election," Karthos said coldly. "She'll do as your queen. Vestar can't interfere with us then. I need to leave for the latest inquisition by the end of the month; you'll be married before then."

He walked out. Suddenly the room spun and Samantha crumpled like a rag doll over Medrhos' arm. She was blessed she wasn't dead.

VII

Lament

The lights twinkled overhead, fascinating Aiyra as she lay on the couch at the low table. She thought they were stars, almost. Talitha sat on the floor, leaning on her husband's knee, watching Aiyra, and Marc was guarding them both.

Dinner hadn't been uneventful – Aiyra had needed to lean on her parents the whole walk to the restaurant. When she had tried to eat, she found out she wasn't quite well and couldn't keep the food down. The restaurant owner, a friend of Talitha's, had kindly brought a sort of solid pudding, blackberry-pink and white, and this she had managed to eat.

Marc looked at the aqua and ivory décor of the place. It was so peaceful he could almost forget the hostile situation they were in. But it was time to go, before Aiyra fell asleep. He lifted her to her feet and walked his family down the stairs and out of the restaurant. Their path led them to a high rocky ground, a park of sorts where many of the enslaved families were enjoying their brief evening freedom and the cool night air. The children ran races around the fountains and splashed in them. The ledge overlooked the city and they could see the church and the plaza.

Marc compared it with the modern-day Zaire and realized that this location in Xirox was the future sight of the governor's palace and the plaza where he had danced with Samantha. He looked again at the church where he and Samantha had taken a 'swim' and commented on the presence of a church.

"Oh, it is not a real church," Aiyra told him sleepily. "It is a mix of things. They have some strange beliefs-"

"It broke off from a Marauder cult," Talitha explained. "It adopted some of our beliefs and made up some strange ones. There is one about free will and magic crystals, or something like that."

"They made it look like a church to get some of us to go in and some stayed," Aiyra sighed.

"Who's 'they'?"

"Oh, the Utharians," his wife answered. "They were the tribe that originally inhabited the planet, and when it was colonized, they bought their way into high places in return for allowing the colonists to stay. They are said to be even worse than the Marauders, though they pretend to serve them. You see, the minerals which Aiyra is forced to mine are turned into a special fuel for the Marauder ships."

Her hand was on Aiyra's shoulder. Her daughter looked up into her eyes, and seeing the pain there, Aiyra kissed her mother's forehead.

"A'ma, I will be alright, you take good care of me. I never let them hurt me – I will be good, A'ma, so please do not worry so!"

"Sweetheart!" Talitha murmured. "My little Aiyra. Will you sit with the children and rest while I speak with your father?"

Aiyra nodded and tread across the stones to sit in the cool fountain mist. Talitha turned to her husband again.

"In turn the Marauders bring them slaves," she continued. "Even now the Utharians hold all the strings; even Daruth is only a puppet, not a master." She turned to him. "If they ordered him to marry me, he would have to kill you, Marc!"

Marc silenced her and said nothing for a few minutes as he looked up at the moon and tried to place this information on the Utharians somewhere where it made sense. Aiyra had never mentioned them, and had indicated that Daruth was fully autonomous. Perhaps she had forgotten? The implant could have disrupted some of her memories.

"I don't think you need to worry about me, Talitha," he said finally. "Whatever happens tomorrow, I love you! I'll do whatever I can. But worry about yourself, Talitha, and our daughter. You are the ones in danger."

He held her hands tightly and brought them to his heart. Talitha thought on this but she became strangely calm.

"Then," she said at last, "we will all be careful. Right now, everything is well, Marc, and we should enjoy it while we can. See, even Aiyra is smiling now because of you." She directed his gaze to their daughter.

Marc managed a smile at this but then his heart felt a strange chill and every little nerve seemed to prick with a needle's pain. The boy she was with – even in the moonlight the silhouette was familiar. The captain pulled his wife after him, while Aiyra was distracted by a younger child who fell and cried. She hurried to pick him up; she was out of earshot. Marc dropped Talitha's hand.

"Konstan?"

The boy jumped and looked at him, his face a puzzle in the dark.

". . . Sir?" He came forward and the moonlight shone on his face and startled blue eyes.

A moment passed. How was he not dead? Was he Konstan in truth? Was he the current Konstan, past, future, present, or merely a look-alike?

"Konstan," Marc said again.

"Captain," the youth replied in a low voice that trembled.

"Are you the real Konstan? What year-?"

"2465 still," he answered. "Though I've lived years here already! You?"

"It should be the same," Marc muttered. "And I have lived years, also. But how, Konstan? We thought you died - Aiyra lost half her heart when we lost you. She has nightmares every night that she could have saved you."

"Poor, poor sweet one!" Konstan groaned. "I don't know."

Silence.

". . . Talitha dies tomorrow. I need you, Konstan." The boy nodded wordlessly and they watched Talitha and Aiyra across the plaza. The girl was wearying again – she needed to return to their home. She'd never have to work in the mines again.

"Be there tomorrow!" Marc whispered, turning to the boy again and clasping his hand. "I can't save either of them, Konstan. But we can save them from suffering alone. Whatever happens, please stay with Aiyra. She needs you now, just as she needs you in time." Konstan nodded.

"I will." He stood alone and watched Marc walk away. The man who bore the Ransomer's cross couldn't ransom his own beloved. . . but legends never die.

~~~

Marc awakened a few hours later in the back room of the apothecary which Talitha and Aiyra called home. It was midnight. Talitha's head was on his shoulder and Aiyra was sleeping next to him. Neither stirred. What had awakened him? He heard a quiet rasping sound out in the apothecary. Gently he lifted Talitha's head and slipped out. He threw on the lights. A man clothed in sable and bronze stood in the doorway, backed by two guards. It could only be Daruth. The two men appraised each other for a few moments in silence.

"You are the husband of Breciendelle."

"I am."

"I wanted to meet you. Where is she?"

"Sleeping."

Daruth looked at him. "Then let her sleep. The palace hall – make sure she's there at dawn." He swung the door shut. The sentence was given. Talitha would die. He had to prepare her for death.

Marc awakened his wife at three in the morning. He motioned for her to follow him and he turned on the lights again. He put his arms around her.

"Daruth was here a few hours ago. You need to be at the palace at dawn." He looked into her upturned face. "Talitha, my love. . .! You will die, and I cannot save you. God has ordained this. There is this grace, at least, that I can warn you."

"I am not afraid, Marc," she said softly, yet clung to him. "But for you and Aiyra, yes!"

"Aiyra will be safe one day," he murmured, his face pressed to her hair. "She was saved and we were reunited . . . And I will be alright, but only because I know you will be with the One Who alone loves you as you deserve."

He was trying to keep his eyes from filling with tears but it couldn't be helped. Talitha pulled away, feeling his shoulders shake.

"Oh, Marc. . ." She took her husband's head in her hands and gently kissed away his tears. "I will only be alright if you will be. Marc, we will get through this together, and I promise, if I go with God, I will bring Him back to you. I will see you again!. . . We only have a few hours, Marc. I need Aiyra – but no, she needs to sleep." She turned her head away, worrying if her daughter would ever be made well again.

"Talitha, what will hurt most will be not being able to say goodbye," Marc said quietly. He entered the chamber and gently shook Aiyra.

"Is it time already?" she asked drowsily. "I do not want to leave you, A'da."

"No, dearest, you'll never work in those mines again," he murmured, picking her up and taking her to her mother. When they explained the situation, Aiyra began to weep and laid her head on her mother's shoulder. But as frightened and as heartbroken as she was, she was soon concentrating on keeping her mother ready for whatever happened. There would be no priest.

~~

"It's time," Marc said soberly a few hours later. Birds had begun to twitter in the darkness outside. He lifted his cloak and wrapped it around his wife and daughter. They leaned on him. No one said anything then. They walked out into the pre-dawn chill.

Their winding path took them around the cliff-face, lined with royal homes. All was shadowed and quiet, with eerie echoes and flickering lamplight. The sky began to lighten ever so slowly until they no longer stumbled over loose stones. They came to a faux alleyway leading as a bottleneck to the fortress gates. A shadow flickered at the yawning mouth ahead of them. Marc halted. He knew this was it.

"Go around, my darlings," he said softly. "I'm afraid I'll be detained. I'll come to you as soon as I can!" He kissed them and sent them running. His cloak quickly masked them in the dark. Into the alley he went.

VIII

Sunrise

Marc stepped into the alley, as foolish as it might seem. If he didn't, however, the two assassins would head for Talitha and Aiyra instead. It was still dark enough that he didn't see the men until they hit him. His back slammed against the cobblestone street, a heavy booted foot on his chest. Marc barely saw the faint silver flash before it was too late. A leaden edged knife, unnecessary perhaps, but it made even the smallest wound lethal.

His reflexes kicked in and he grabbed the assassin's wrist, pulling him forward, and kicked the man in the shins, causing him to trip and barely miss Marc's throat. Marc had only a split second to roll away and get on his feet before the other assassin was on top of him, quickly joined by the first.

Marc was grateful that his time spent training for the fleet had included combat and self-defense. Even though he was a bit rusty, he had practiced often on the *Lumenara*. Without it he'd already be dead. Trying to fight a professional assassin, let alone two, was nearly an impossible task. His hair was wet with sweat despite the chill and his muscles were aching from the relentless flurry of attack. Neither assassin was tired.

The sky grew a little lighter and Marc noticed that the second assassin was a woman. Which wasn't significant except for the fact that as they fought, he noticed she was too strong and too confident for her own good. He feigned slipping in the mud and the male assassin, presumably the woman's brother, grabbed his collar and forced him against the wall. Said wall was of a porous rock, weathered enough that the outer layers were crumbling.

Marc watched as the woman drew a shock blade and leapt at him, her arm coming down in a sweeping arc – Marc slammed his elbow into his captor's ribcage, freeing himself, and sending him tumbling down a flight of stairs to a sunken home in the alley. The woman's momentum carried her blade deep into the wall, rattling her body and stunning her for a moment.

Amused, Marc grasped her shoulder, pulling her hand free from the blade's wrapped hilt, and tipped her into the nearest dumpster, slamming the lid. Two down. He double-checked that the other assassin was still out of commission. He was solidly unconscious from hitting his head on the iron balustrade.

Marc's brain tried to get back into gear. What was he doing again? The cold breeze shook him awake and he felt a touch on his arm. Marc jumped and looked to see a man who was vaguely familiar. A glimpse of golden metal beneath white and gray; he looked at the man's face.

"Talitha and your daughter need you," the stranger said gently. "Marc, don't be afraid. There is only one path you can take. It has been decided. Whether you will walk it is your choice to make. Comfort Talitha, then you must run, for time is running out. Samantha needs you, and without you, many will die. Go now, warrior. It is time for the beginning of the end of this slavery."

Marc, bewildered, turned as he heard a shout brought down on the wind. Without pausing to think, he ran. He flung the gate's guards aside and crashed through the great doors while others moved to stop him. The throne room fell away before him as Daruth snatched up the sword and cast the blow – Marc screamed something – it took until hours afterward to realize what he had said.

Vives in gladio peribit! He leapt forward and caught Talitha as she fell, blood on her neck. His cry had shifted the blow; she did not die instantly as Aiyra had remembered. In the chaos that ensued, as the slaves rose in rebellion, Aiyra was dragged from the throne room, Konstan following; Daruth was struck down and Marc swept Talitha into his arms and carried her to the safety of the grassy knoll outside that fell over the cliff below.

He knelt, shielding Talitha with his body, cradling her in his arms and trying to keep the wound from tearing open any further. There was nothing he could do for Aiyra; all he could do was keep Talitha from dying alone. He didn't heed the cries nor the victory that soon began to spread throughout the city as the people arose to avenge the queen they had loved.

"Marc!" Talitha whispered. Her white dress was quickly turning blood-red. The color had faded from her face. Marc knew he only had a moment. He drew her closer so she could lay her hand on his heart as she was wont to do.

"Listen," Talitha whispered. "Let me see your face." Her fingers weakly grasped the cross that Aiyra loved. Marc covered her hand with his. Talitha's eyes opened again, clear and smiling.

"Marc. . . my love! Thank you - for giving me a life so beautiful. . . I never thought I could have lived it."

She clutched at the cross as her body shook but she still looked up as Marc held her quietly. He was ready and the pain was dull deep within him. It didn't show. Talitha continued to struggle to speak before time ran out.

"Thank you for our daughter - thank you for giving me you! Oh, all that I never could have asked for, God gave me. . . I would not avoid this death if it meant losing Him and not saying God-speed to you. . . You think I saved you. . . but you have saved me more than once. Without you I fear I never would have been ready. Thank you for coming for us – it was not in vain, my love, though you may lose us both. My Daystar, my lover, my king! O, Marc! Would that I could say the things that must be said, oh if I have ever hurt you-or Aiyra-or anyone-"

"Oh, Talitha! Hush, no man or woman in this world has ever been hurt by you. Don't cry! Soon Aiyra and I will come to you and nothing shall part us . . . save that God might not let you go long enough to let us hold you again. I wouldn't blame Him."

He kissed her as her breath began to fade and he held her hands tight. Her eyes were shut and she struggled to live; but she gave up knowing that there was nothing more she could say. She had Marc with her, at least, to guide her. Maybe Aiyra wasn't there, but she'd see her daughter soon enough.

Be with her! Marc raised his head to see the sunlight streaming in. Talitha opened her eyes. The sun had risen. A smile like no other graced Talitha's face as she gazed into it.

"*Jesu, Rex, Maria, Regina,*" her lips moved and her hands slipped from his. She fell back in Marc's grieving embrace. But he had no fear. Talitha would never need to see the sun set. She was home.

IX

Eldritch

Days were passing swiftly now. Autumn was growing redder, and Mal'lon's great winter would soon be there. Already the deep seas to the south were freezing over, little by little, and the fjords' cliff faces were creepingly, gradually hung with sheets of ice. Almost without the bubbling excitement and hubbub that usually accompanied great weddings, the preparations were being carried out.

Finest wine was brought from the sunny planet of Tusca, rare fish from the still-warm northern oceans of Peliva, and delicacies from the garden-covered moons of Athelnir, with its vineyards, caves, farms, orchards, and mills. Jewels, silks, glass goblets, tapestries, and flowering vines were imported from the richest planets in history.

The buildings of the city were never whiter, the streets never brighter with their cleansing and white-washing and festooned lamps like glittering stars and gems. Flowers began to be seen growing everywhere in raspberry, blush, plum, and gold, and lush vines formed an airy ceiling high above the courtyards.

Samantha spent each morning looking out from her balcony to see how close things were coming. She could feel her heart aching, something etching deeply into her soul, searching for someone she loved.

Samantha closed her eyes and wondered if those blue eyes were filled with tears, or did they smile with the sun looking into Talitha's face? But something prodded her with guilt.

No, Marc would not forget her, even for his joy if he had Talitha at his side. He was her captain, and to him present duty would come before what had been in the past. . . what may well never be possible again. Samantha sighed and rubbed her burned arm.

She had slowly recovered from the incident with the fire bracelet. She still wasn't sure if they had meant for it to explode or not. Maybe the test had been whether she could fight and win. Her recovery had been no thanks to Karthos. He tormented her and pushed her to her limits and past them, every chance he got.

For example, on one occasion he had Samantha's chief handmaiden and companion, Silvestra, lead her into one of the sunken cellars. Silvestra thought it was for choosing a few pieces of ancient jewelry for the wedding; but when she stepped outside, Karthos slammed the door shut and locked Samantha, who was still very weak, in the soundproof and escape-proof room. No one found her until two in the morning when the heavy rains had already half-flooded the cellar.

Medrhos, looking furious, had guided her back to her room. She wasn't sure if his annoyance was with her or if Silvestra had finally escaped Karthos' trick on her (she had been unceremoniously dumped into the laundry pile and buried) and had told the King all about it. But Medrhos had been unable to hide his anxiety over her, as he had ordered Silvestra to care for her most tenderly, and promptly called a physician to tend to the future Queen.

When such things were done to Samantha, trinkets would suddenly show up in her room by way of Silvestra and Coran, who was her guard now that Karthos was present; but it was always done secretly, for, of course, Karthos mustn't know. The man was far darker in thought than Samantha had known him to be, and this instance was only one of many.

In any event, the entire process had the desired effect of stretching the engineer's limits, until she was strong enough to carry whatever Karthos threw at her. She caught him smiling proudly at her occasionally. It was much like what he had done with Medrhos.

The Marauder King had grown harsh and cold once more and hardly stopped each morning to bother her for a greeting. He took every chance to display his power, ruthlessness, and abilities when Karthos was near, setting off on brutal hunting expeditions, after which he would display grotesque trophies of dangerous beasts, terrorize a sub-kingdom, or twist a treaty until he was the only one who benefited from it.

Meanwhile, Karthos would nod with pleasure at his grandson's antics and then verbally slap Samantha until the King was white with fury. It was as though Karthos was trying to get the upper hand and continue that 'legendary training' he had famously given his grandson many years before. Unable to stop Karthos' maltreatment of the engineer, Medrhos would explosively turn on the servants or run out on an all-day scouting party until the pressure was off.

In general, however, he was merely a block of ice – for the most part. In the same moment he would be stern, but almost rejoicing at the wedding preparations like a young boy. This only came to the surface in those rare moments when he stepped down from his duties and played with Gelert in the garden, and this only when Karthos' eyes were elsewhere. The old man watched him with a cruel hawk's gaze, smiling at the wedding chains being prepared for the pair.

Samantha could feel the strange mix of mutual hatred and respect between the two men; but she would smile, a trifle wistfully, watching Medrhos and Gelert at play while she stroked the cat, whom she had named Lyona, and was fitted the thousandth time for a wedding dress.

Jewels, furs, feathers, and flowers were scattered thickly everywhere. Medrhos was giving her everything she desired, or anything he *thought* she desired. She would have been more amused by a child's electric kit. Though, she did catch herself admiring some of the mess, while she only too happily let her handmaids play with the trinkets before they were stored away.

Samantha paced her suddenly emptied room restlessly when the gown was finally approved and sent for.

The wedding was in two weeks' time; finally, she could get some fresh air. But anywhere she went, Karthos was sure to follow. She hadn't visited the slaves in a week, and she knew they were looking for her. If she went in disguise... she quickly called in Silvestra, who allowed her to borrow her only other outfit of rough brown and burgundy.

Samantha then slipped out, blending in with the servants who were heading to the market. The children were waiting and ran to greet her, begging for a story. She sat down with them and told them tales she had woven for Konstan and Aiyra while working, and some ancient Earth fables which even Medrhos had wanted to hear.

This was one of the few joys Samantha had; that and the secret Mass that a priest came and said for all of them. When he turned towards them for the homily, Samantha stifled a gasp. She rushed up to him as soon as Mass was over.

"My lord! I mean, Father-" It was Ransomme. He smiled.

"Yes, it is Father now. I was in seminary, almost ordained, when I saw you last. I heard you were here, Ms. Anselle. I've wanted to see you, but it is rare that I can slip away for a mere 'walk.'" He laughed and then drew her aside and listened to her tale.

He confirmed the story of the *Delta's* capture by the false signal and mercenaries, and how the captives had been transported instantly via a vortex like the one into which Marc had vanished. He nodded to himself as she explained the situation with Medrhos and her fears.

"I don't know what God is calling me to do," Samantha ended. "The only thing I know is that He wants me to marry; but who? If Marc is with his wife. . . it leaves Medrhos, I guess." She looked up at him, not really thinking he could aid her. His advice was sound.

"Daughter, many great saints are women who suffered marriage issues. Some managed to save their husband through the closeness of their example. This may be your path. It remains to be seen where Marc and Medrhos' paths end. Live in the moment, Samantha. You are not your past, nor your future. God is. Every man's path is lined with angels; they will help you to get to where you are going. Do they not serve the One Who paid the price for us all? God gave them the stars to be their torches that we may know that we are never alone. Do not fear, Samantha. One way or another, you'll know what to do when the time comes." He raised his hand and blessed her before slipping away.

Samantha returned to the palace, forcing herself to consider that she might need to wed the Marauder King. When it came down to it, like becoming a Marauder, it wasn't the worst that could happen.

Despite her sarcasm when speaking with Medrhos, she did consider slavery to be the worst option.

Knowing Karthos, if she rebelled against the match or otherwise dismayed him, he would see to it that she would either die an agonizing death in slavery, darkness, and slime, or he'd somehow cause her to lead others to their death. She knew that she could straighten Medrhos out in time; she had already seen some positive effects from her presence.

The main problem was, again, Karthos. When he left things would be better. Could she lead Medrhos to safety and pray for a way to end Karthos' terrorizing – or did she need a hero? She already had received the One and Only. Whether He chose a human hero to save her, and whether she could save Medrhos, and whether there was time, He was not ready to tell her. So, she could relax. She laughed to herself.

She knew that she could handle Medrhos and that he wouldn't hurt her – much. And it was clear that he wouldn't be too much of a disturbance since he didn't believe in relationships that were obviously close.

She thought of Marc's goodness and gentleness, and the fact that he loved her. A man who had been married to the most beautiful and wonderful woman in the galaxy who could still love only an engineer – his sorrow didn't stop his heart from wanting to protect her. Her own heart melted. But who needed her more? If Marc was with Talitha, then he was safe. Yet he needed to get back to Aiyra.

She entered her room and pulled off her cloak. Her watch beeped as she switched out of her peasant garb. Medrhos wanted her in the armory. She grabbed her gloves and cape and headed out. She had to cross a courtyard to get to the armory; the sun was setting and the wind brought a chill with it. Medrhos was waiting, arms folded and sword at his side. It was an old-fashioned one; she wondered why.

"There you are," he said with a slight smile. "I hope you enjoyed that long walk."

The engineer wondered how he knew, but said nothing. The King answered anyway.

"Karthos has been keeping track of that signal on your wrist," he said, examining a second blade. He tossed it to her and she belted it at her waist. "He asked me to turn it off but to get you an RFID chip . . . so that we don't lose you, of course." He was clearly being sarcastic.

"I know you so well," Samantha said lightly, parrying as he experimentally struck out at her. "You won't do it. And you know it'd be easier if you just put me in chains. . ."

They began dueling on the platform that ran outside and overlooked a quiet swimming pool and the valley below. Medrhos took a second to answer.

"The man who chains you will die," he replied. "And I shut down Karthos' ability to track you."

"So, he knows I was out, or doesn't he? And technically you put me in chains, Medrhos."

"Yes, he does. And I haven't seen you try to escape." He lunged and Samantha leapt aside and slid down the stairway railing. He jumped down and dueled her alongside the pool.

"Because I know you can track me," Samantha replied in between strikes.

"Then turn off the signal."

Samantha evaded his sword and lightly struck his arm with the flat of her blade. "I don't feel like it," she returned. "But I do feel like turning you off!" She tripped him as he moved around her and down he went into the pool with a splash, leaving Samantha laughing.

Medrhos came up and rolled his eyes but they both froze when they heard an eerie laugh carried on the wind. It was the sort of laugh you might expect to come from the haunted skull of an insane man whose jaw moved quicker than he as his eyes flipped in his head. It was the laugh of tyrants' graveyards, pirates' shipyards, and the orchestration of nightmares.

In an instant, Medrhos was out of the water and at Samantha's side, alert and tense. Samantha, feeling a creepy chill running through her and almost feeling the presence of something in that courtyard, looked at the man who stood beside her, eyes and senses straining as he stared into the night. He was protecting her. Suddenly Samantha felt strangely safe. The wind breathed a comforting sigh and they heard nothing more. Slowly the fearful presence faded. Medrhos was the first to break the silence.

"You need to get inside." Without asking, he took her hand, grabbed both swords, and pulled her up the stairs. They shut the armory doors and Medrhos then remembered he was dripping wet.

Samantha offered him her cloak as a towel and he smiled – it was almost a real smile for once. Then they realized Karthos was right next to them. Medrhos inhaled sharply and drew himself to his full height, bracing himself for whatever scathing remark his grandfather had prepared for him.

"Well, you could have fought better," Karthos said bluntly. He turned to Samantha. "And you could have fought worse. Try this next time." He tossed something to her and she caught it.

The tiny jewel-encrusted scabbard just fit within her palm. She drew out the hilt and watched as the paper-thin blade grew and revealed its murderous jagged edge. Her face paled when she realized that it was one of the deadliest and ancient Marauder weapons, carried by queens and assassins alike for its swift and easy use. The blade could be molded into any shape and it could be filled with the most lethal poisons which would be discharged in the first blow. She could never use it.

Wait – was he asking her to use it if necessary, or use it on Medrhos? She raised her wide eyes and glanced at them both but neither wore any particular expression other than annoyance with each other. She said nothing, put it back in its sheath, and pinned it at her waist.

"Now, go." Karthos turned to Medrhos and ignored her.

"No, Samantha, wait in the hall," Medrhos said sharply. He turned away. Samantha shook her head but complied. It wasn't her fault that she heard everything that Karthos said.

"…Listen, Medrhos. You know she's as dangerous as any member of the Fleet would be. I never told you that she's the reason we went to Almedra. I knew that she could make or break our people. I knew that she'd serve on a Vestar ship and she'd mean something to them. We can use her to block the Fleet's efforts against us. She'll be a queen that they cannot stop. . . Keep a constant eye on her; we can't risk losing her as your queen. And get that RFID chip! I lost my ability to track her. I don't trust that girl. She's too free."

"I know!" Medrhos snapped. "And no, I won't! Let her have some privacy. She's not one of your whipped dogs." Karthos hissed softly.

"Never mind. Just get her to the altar. As soon as you're married, I want the ships moving. We have a few forward payments I'd like to make."

"And I have a few problems with everything you just said," Medrhos said through gritted teeth. "First, I'd like to have a honeymoon. Second, I'll decide whether we're moving. Third, I'm not using Samantha! And finally, there is only one king here, and it's not you." He stormed out into the hall and stopped short when he saw the look in Samantha's eyes.

"Oh for-" he shut himself up and grabbing Samantha's arm, walked her back to her room. He stopped just long enough to ask, "If you hear anything-"

"I know."

Medrhos nodded slowly and then shook himself. In a moment he was back to his usual manner and Samantha straightened. The King had as many faces to him, just as Aiyra did. Which was right? The arrogance, wrath, and cunning that surfaced most often was logically his true face. But then what did his gentle episodes mean?

"Don't have any nightmares now, *ancilla*," he smirked, and left with his mocking bow. But the thread of thought in Samantha's mind led to a whirlwind stream of nightmares.

Marc dead, murdered for saving Talitha.

Marc crying over Talitha's body.

Marc in chains.

Marc spending his life trying to find her, only to find Medrhos' queen instead. Marc spending his life alone, lost even without Aiyra.

Marc lost in a snowstorm, calling her name. He was being beaten down by the winds but he kept on blindly, knowing that she needed him. Samantha struggled to call to him but the wind silenced her. Marc's body gave up on him – he fell in the snow.

Samantha tried to scream and ford through the snow but her skirts got caught and dragged her down. She couldn't reach him! The snow was burying him – he vanished from sight and the storm blinded her. A laughing skull burned through the blizzard, eyes winking at her. She had veritably killed him.

"Marc!"

Samantha started up in her bed with a strangled cry. The balcony door had banged open in the wind of a brewing storm and she was chilled through. She half expected to see a laughing skull sitting there in the doorway, but there was only the moon.

Samantha glanced down at her wrists and saw a faint silver glow beating steadily. Her heart stopped pounding and she felt that sweet relief that always comes after a false scare. But was she killing Marc somehow? Was his memory of her holding him down? Something was telling her to pray for him. She shut her eyes tight as her heart rate began to hasten again.

Finally, letting out her breath, she got up to shut the door and curtains, turning the lights on dim. Lyona walked up to her, purring, and followed her into bed. Samantha smiled when the cat climbed up to her, and curling up, rested her head on the engineer's arm.

"I suppose you belong to someone from the *Delta* and I'll have to return you," she murmured fondly. "But I'm glad I have you for right now." She hugged her and fell asleep with the thought of escaping for Marc's sake. . . somehow.

X

Glitter

Samantha took a sip of the shimmering water in her chalice and grimaced. She had met with Medrhos in the morning parlor at sunrise; both felt the mutual pull to be together awaiting Karthos' usual morning arrival, and were taking whatever light breakfast they could stomach beforehand; light by Marauder standards, at any rate.

There were dense date bars, yogurt equally so dense that Samantha was sure it would break her plate, a wild intergalactic species of dragon's eye fruit, and Medrhos' favorite, down-sized spicy quiches wrapped with bacon in lieu of a crust.

The only options for a beverage was a coffee brewed darker than Karthos' intents and the strange water Samantha was now attempting to drink. The glass and rose-gold urn it was served in showed off the faint shimmering specks of emerald, copper, and peach within the liquid. She had chosen this suspicious substance after the coffee had scorched and turned her stomach, nearly rewiring her brain at the same time with its concentrated caffeine.

Samantha had been amazed to see that Medrhos was staying hydrated for once, indulging in the water as well. It was, in fact, water from the sacred aquifer that ran below Mal-lon's surface, and was kept only for the Marauder people. Its health benefits weren't given to slaves or anyone outside of Marauder birth, except by the King's permission, and thus it was a staple at the Marauder table.

"I don't care for the taste of this water," Samantha said, putting down her goblet. Medrhos was drinking his with a bored look, clearly wishing that it were anything fermented.

"It's the minerals from the caverns below the city," he replied. "You don't need to drink it if you don't like it. I mean, you have to. I mean, no! You don't." He was scowling at the wall.

Karthos made his entrance at that moment, erasing Samantha's questioning expression with some derogatory remark about warriors and women swapping breakfast as he promptly took possession of the remaining date bars and shoved Samantha out of her seat.

Her suspicions were already well aroused, however. As dire was her need to escape for Marc's sake, she was still formulating a plan and surely had enough time to see the source of this strange water for herself.

"Samantha!" Karthos shocked her so sharply the girl's hand knocked the goblet to the floor. It smashed and the girl frowned to see that the liquid seemed to gel, glue-like, in contact with the air and stone. Karthos smirked.

"My *dear* future granddaughter, it's dreadfully unbecoming to jump when I'm speaking to you. Do try to be all ears. I want you to come for a walk with me so we can tell you how to correct yourself before you belong to Medrhos. For one thing, your shadow looks better than you, so we'll have to fix that."

"Medrhos!" Samantha fixed her eyes on the king sweetly, drawing him out of his flaring gaze aimed at a spot above Karthos' head. "My *dear* future husband, I'd like to take a walk by myself."

Karthos made an indignant sound preparing to lace another proverbial dart with poison. Medrhos' gaze slid to his grandfather's face and then back to Samantha. A twist of a smile tugged on one corner of his mouth.

"You are a Marauder now, Samantha, but not yet Queen. You are under *my* guardianship." Just when Karthos thought all was well, his grandson added, "So take a walk alone if you please."

Samantha abandoned them at once. She had no real knowledge of the caverns, save for the one she had been thrown into from the throne room pool. Would she have to dive into it? Surely there was some other entrance. It struck her that Silvestra might know of the place where the water was collected, and if not, she knew that her handmaid could obtain the information from Coran.

Indeed, it was only a matter of minutes before the girl's sweetness had convinced Coran to show Samantha even more than what she had asked. He led her to the hall of the ancients, a grand hall adjacent to the throne room, and which Samantha had never entered.

Tapestries and pennants of jet-black and red hung on the walls, draping from the soaring ceiling nearly to the floor. The north wall was built to enshrine a dark granite fountain that bubbled softly as it spilled into an angular pool. A pool, Samantha realized, that was shaped not unlike the crystal Medrhos had shown her.

"This is where we take the water for those in the palace," Coran stated. "As for those in the cities and elsewhere, there are aquifers running all throughout Mal-lon's crust, so each village and town has its own place for acquiring the water they need. Here in the city there are two fountains that carry this water; all others and all the wells contain everyday water, without the sacred benefits."

"But where does it come from?" Samantha pressed. "Why is it different? Surely it must have a source."

Coran hesitated. "There is," he admitted. "I shouldn't tell you but -" he looked at her closely. "The source lies deep in the mountain below the palace. If you wish to reach it you'll have to take the passageway behind the throne."

He saw her obvious confusion and waved her after him with a half amused, half frustrated frown. The wall behind the throne, with the carven thorns and rushing sheets of water, jutted outward to accentuate the throne. The carvings masked a narrow entryway on either side of the wall.

"I cannot take you down," Coran said, looking away. "It is a long walk, besides."

Samantha refused to be deterred. "I appreciate you showing me this, Coran. Will you have to tell Medrhos?"

Coran was still gazing away from her. His eyes moved restlessly across the doorway. "Probably." He glanced back at her.

"I understand. If it's any risk to you. . .." Coran shook his head. He and Medrhos were close. If he bent the rules Medrhos was always there to hide the fact they had ever been touched. And it wasn't like Medrhos had no knowledge of how persuasive Samantha could be. He almost smiled as Samantha, reassured, lost no further time in investigating the new lead. He could give her a few minutes. But if she reached the end before he confessed. . . his guardianship of her couldn't allow it. His eyes narrowed and he strode off in search of his liege.

Meanwhile, Samantha found herself at the mouth of a wide, downward sloping tunnel of sharp incline. Ancient and modern lights alike marked the walls, and the floor had been rippled into a natural staircase by the floods of the ancient rainy seasons and many footfalls. There was a guide post on the wall, written in the Marauder tongue. The only word Samantha could understand was *crystlvanya*, 'crystal cavern.'

Her heart beat a little faster. So, she might find the source of the water *and* the source of the crystals. She'd have to be careful what she touched. There was no telling just how quickly Coran would alert Medrhos of Samantha's doings, so she hastened downward.

When she reached the bottom of the first slope she knew she had found what she was seeking. A maze of caverns stretched miles in every direction beneath the rock, some large enough to contain a massive warship like the *Harbinger*, others scarcely big enough for Gelert.

Rivers and streams wound through the passageways, having carved so deeply into the stone that only narrow ledges were left to walk upon, raised high above the water. Rivulets ran down the walls, and the only sounds in the distance were the continued gurgling of the waterways and the roar of a distant waterfall.

At first, there were handrails, bridges in some places, and occasional lights along the walls as she made her way through chambers of heated lagoons used for therapeutic spas and swimming pools, and other storerooms for cheese, aged honey, and mead.

It wasn't long before all of these signs of life began to seem more and more ancient, and more and more rare. The new electric lights gave way to ancient crystal lamps, the handrails ceased to exist, and the path was worn more and more slick with age. She discovered caves that had never seen the light of day or even a flashlight, some that glowed with phosphorescent moss, and many in various stages of drowning.

It was quiet and grew cooler the deeper Samantha ventured. The dark stone struggled to reflect the beams from her watch's flashlight. She found hardly a sign of life save strange, strange marks on the walls at the various twists, turns, and intersections. The girl ran her fingertips over them with the creeping feeling that she had seen them before. She frowned upon seeing certain familiar shapes, though half worn away. Her skull began to prick with a chill.

The passage threw an echoing laugh up at her and for just a moment, Samantha thought it might be the same ghostly one she had been hearing, but it was only the voices of three approaching members of Medrhos' guard. Their voices were distorted by the presence of the many walls and waters.

"They mustn't see me too quickly," Samantha muttered, wondering if Medrhos already knew, and leapt up the wall to a narrow ledge that crept along overhead, with breaks in the walls as though it were a natural, though micro-sized, colonnade. Her back and neck were aching before long, and the girl was glad to see the end of it. She perched on the high ledge, looking down at the continuing ribbons of river and rock.

Were all of these rivers and streams the source of the water, or was there one sacred location? She hadn't been noticing the same glimmering effect in the water, but considering the space between her level and the river below, she could easily have missed it in the dim lighting.

The path sloped ahead and extended into another chamber which promised to be a more comfortable than the one she was currently in, so she dropped from her ledge. She nearly slid into the channel, the stone was so tractless beneath her feet.

There was something decidedly different about this cavern. Here it showed signs of ancient civilization once more. The walls and ceiling had been roughly straightened into more of a rectangular shape, with four lamps marking the corners of the room. They cast a subtly orange light which caught on every bump of stone and threw a grotesque shadow Samantha's way. A rock pool too, had been carved into a rectangular basin, and the river flowed in and out, the continuation vanishing into the wall.

"Oh, strung webs and stardust, just my luck!" Samantha groaned. "This doorway better lead to somewhere where I can follow that water, or else I may as well get to escaping." But she paused; she still needed to verify whether this was the same water she was hunting down or not.

Samantha glanced into the pool's depths, and in the lamplight saw more than the glimmer she sought. Time specters like wisps of smoke seemed to swim in and out of her vision as though souls had once perished and taken possession of the stone. The engineer shuddered, her heart growing more and more disturbed by the minute, and hurried onward.

The exiting doorway returned her to the central tunnel which was jarring in the obvious signs of frequent use, compared to where she had been. Samantha glanced up and down the tunnel. There were no signs of any visitors so she was free to cautiously make her way down the slope. The air grew crisper the farther she went, ironically passing evidences of ancient magma, steam vents, and burning saunas.

The sound of running water was no longer audible; there was only a low, faint roar that seemed to come from deeper underground.

The lights continued to line the walls, changing to an icy shade to match the chill on Samantha's skin.

"Why didn't I bring a wrap when it's the demise of autumn?" she muttered, rubbing her arms and peering around the next bend. The drone was increasing and she was beginning to hear an occasional low, crackling, settling groan, as though the stones were shifting with the weight above them and the gravity below.

If the path didn't end soon – her mind was continually crowded with the fearful shadow of those specters and her nightmare about Marc. Was this wasted time, and was she endangering him? She almost turned back but she was sure she must be close to what she was seeking.

"If it's not around the next bend," she promised herself, "I'll put my escape plan into the works."

As she continued, she began to see that the light on the walls seemed refracted, and in shades of rose and violet cast over by a stain of cold blue. Everything seemed azure despite the white light of the lamps there. Something around the next bend was causing this strange refraction, and that raised Samantha's hopes that she didn't, after all, have to turn back early.

What greeted her eyes was not what she could have imagined, even by the name crystal cavern. Three caves branched off one another, far smaller than may she had seen. Freakishly massive crystals, many times her height in length, fell across the cavern like the bracing bones of some preternatural, yet terrestrial monster.

The very walls scintillated with a pulsating throb, like that of an unnatural heartbeat, for every millimeter of stone was covered with thousands of growing, glistening crystals. The pulsing light rippled through a rainbow of ruby, amber, amethyst, opal, and coral, and when Samantha hesitantly took a step down, her boots were drenched to the ankle in unseen water, invisible with a floor of crystal beneath. This reflected the blue light. She quickly stepped back and found the narrow channel that led across the water.

In the alcove of the main cave was a pedestal that drew shudders through Samantha's arm. It was identical to the one from her trial, except instead of a bracelet it bore a small bowl of obsidian, clamped by a skeletal, clawed hand. Water came slushing out of the base of the pedestal amid the deep, earthen rumble and the softly frustrating, continuous plinking of water droplets oozing from the crystal ceiling.

As Samantha watched, she saw each drop carried another speck of crystalline glitter into the vanishing pool below. So, the crystal caverns *were* the source. Samantha felt her heart tremble a little studying the scene.

That basin – those thousands and thousands, dare she say millions of twinkling stones – Samantha found her feet slipping down the incline into the cave as her eyes locked on the spinning beat of the cavern's heart.

So many crystals, so many lights! The droning grew louder and louder with a crackling rumble and the lights were spinning faster and faster –

Samantha stumbled into the pool, hardly able to see as the pressure was closing in on her ears and eyes. She could hear a reverberating laugh coming up out of the walls – she was spinning dizzily, trying not to let the now glowing grimace in the crystals get behind her back as her breath seemed to tear in her lungs as though she were drowning. That face – those eyes – that laugh!

"No!" Samantha barely heard herself shriek as the wall behind the pedestal seemed to peel back like a rhinestone decal, beginning to reveal something she didn't want to see.

"Samantha!"

Samantha's head snapped backwards as she was grabbed from behind and the spinning and pressure halted as she stared up into the face of Medrhos.

"Why did you come here?" he growled in a voice so low that she didn't have to guess at his emotion. Her breath was coming hard and fast; she only closed her eyes a moment as her dizziness faded away. But then her gaze darted to the wall and the King's did as well as he held her back against him.

The opening rift faded and Samantha was left unsure as to whether she had ever seen it. Yet she could feel something gnawing and clawing at her mind, worse than the specters and the symbols on the wall, dreadfully similar to the voice that had interrogated her from the bracelet.

Desperation seized her and she shoved Medrhos backwards. The King jerked her up the ramp, dragging her back up the passageway. He halted only once they had rounded the curtain of thorns and were standing in the sunlight of the throne room.

"That was dangerous," he said. "I never want you wandering those caverns again. They are sacred to our people, and while you are becoming one of us, they were not meant for your Almedran blood. The last time one of your bloodline was discovered down there. . . those crystals can be vampiric, Samantha. It took quite a bit of time to repair the damage done, but rest assured, I would not let one of your people perish in my domain or anywhere else, if it be in my power."

He released her arm, which he had been gripping so tightly that Samantha had to wonder whether she had accumulated another bruise.

"Now we must be swift, for if *Karthos* ever finds out what you just did -" He froze, listening to a familiar, heavy-heeled step coming towards the hall. "You certainly know how to pick your timing, Samantha."

"Quick!" Samantha shoved him in front of the throne and away from the hidden doorway. "Pretend you're teaching me something!"

Medrhos cast about in desperation, then pulled his blaster from its holster and rapidly rifted a vortex at the head of the pool. "So! You're in danger and you're alone, and you see a portal. Do you jump into it?"

"Yes!"

Medrhos struck his forehead. "No! Definitely not! It's not like it'll be me! What even -? Try again."

Samantha rolled her eyes. "Well, I would if it led anywhere away from *you*."

Medrhos growled under his breath. "You're not helping," he hissed. "Yes, and what if it takes you to hell, little Catholic girl?"

"Pfft," Samantha laughed, ignoring the batlike figure of Karthos haunting the doorway. "Nice thing about hell, you can't get there via portal. You're pretty good at breaking the rules, though, so you'd best watch yourself!"

"Now, that's the most accurate thing I've heard come out of your mouth." Karthos advanced and Samantha turned to meet him.

"Oh, so saying that you're a mangy-looking bird of prey that's unfit to teach Medrhos *anything* doesn't count? My mistake!"

And Samantha sailed out, leaving both men staring after her in a mix of consternation and complete concordance. Her heart was still beating fast after her scare. More than ever, she needed to ensure Marc's safety. More than ever, she knew how dire it was that she find the key to saving Medrhos.

XI

Futile

Samantha entered Medrhos' and Karthos' presence the next morning as serenely as though all was well. Neither man would have guessed that she had a rigged-up override device in her pocket, one which she knew would enable her to easily borrow one of the aerospeeders kept in the city spaceport.

Not only had she salvaged the pieces and costume for the project from the military cast-off pile, but she had swiped an unmarked ID card from the office and used her etching pen to create the proper keycode on it. It would let her into the hanger and get her through any security checks. The benefits of being an engineer were nothing to be taken for granted. She'd escape that evening when half a dozen soldiers would head out on patrol.

For now, she stood before the king and his grandfather, smiling away in amusement as they questioned her on wedding preparations, informed her of the guest list and the proper protocol, and planned on what name to give her when she was formally initiated before the wedding ceremony.

Samantha just agreed with whatever they said, saving the knowledge as mere items of interest for later. They were in the great hall kept for great feasts, almost ballroom-esque in style. It was being decorated with lights and gold and silver garlands, candles, and rainforest flowers that spilled everywhere, carpeting the ground with their petals. Samantha looked around and began to idly wonder what sort of wedding it could even be. There was no church, and Medrhos was certainly no Christian.

Medrhos snapped his fingers in her face and she jumped. Both men wore the same annoyed look. How similar they could be at times!

"Try to pay attention, *ancilla*," the King said sharply.

"That's a good name," Karthos commented.

Samantha consented to listen to the veritable history lesson which, last she had heard, was on ancient queens, the powers, laws, and responsibilities given them, the symbolism of their clothing, and the age-old diadem and gems they wore. But now it was about the wedding itself.

"Marauder weddings generally consist of several ceremonies before the couple passes through two fires, constituting the making of the first bond," Medrhos was saying. "But since we know that you'll find a way out on the grounds that your race, your religion, that is, believes only in one particular ceremony, we have arranged for one Father Ransomme to perform it. . . do you know of him?"

His classic sarcasm, Samantha thought as she watched Karthos' face. Both had agreed for once, and looked pleased with themselves.

"Why yes, I do," Samantha said sweetly. "But what you don't know is that a forced marriage never counts as anything but sacrilege. . .I expect you know what that means?"

Medrhos eyed her. "Watch yourself, Samantha. I'll let you go now," he said reluctantly. "You need to memorize what we've told you. I'll come by and quiz you later." His eyes twinkled when he saw the flash of mild alarm on Samantha's face as she turned to go. He gave his signature bow and Samantha exited.

She felt that she couldn't wait for the evening patrol, yet there was no earlier chance. She spent her day resting and waiting for Medrhos to come by and quiz her. He never did. Samantha thought of various ways to save the slaves. All of them involved stealing one of the Marauder ships with its ability to navigate through time, and that was a task too great for her to do on her own. Perhaps she could get aid from one of those terrorized kingdoms.

Samantha wandered the gardens and the palace to avoid the obvious strangeness of her spending an entire day in her room. She then returned to get a bit of sleep.

It was nearing five when she awoke, and the sun would set soon. The patrol would likely be heading out in a quarter of an hour so that each soldier could reach his post before nightfall. The number of men always varied based on who felt like going for a ride, for the aerospeeders were held in relatively the same light as a good motorcycle back home. Yes, motorcycles – of a sort – had even become popular on Almedra.

Samantha took a deep breath and double-checked that she had her card, override device, and the few odds and ends she might need to aid her disguise. With that, she headed down to the observation platform overlooking the spaceport. She had made a point of coming there every evening, because it had the best view of the sunset. It wouldn't be strange for anyone to see her there. She idly watched the sky and then slipped into a long unused utility room, intended for scrapping the following week (the beams were falling and many electric wires exposed, no longer a danger due to Samantha's skill, but no one knew that).

She located the uniform she had stashed away. It was a cast-off due to having been returned to the military supplier with a few rips in the coat. These the engineer had skillfully mended. She put it on, tucking her now-braided hair into the cap and surveying herself in a shiny piece of durasteel.

The wide-collared coat fell to the thigh and breeches tucked neatly into knee-high boots. A wide leather belt, which was joined to armor plating underneath like the leather shoulder stripes and lower layer of the coat, helped to make her look more like a young, skinny soldier than a girl playing dress-up with her brother. She darkened her eyebrows with a miscellaneous piece of charcoal in her pocket, and pulled the cap lower over her eyes. It was imperfect, but good enough. Or so she hoped.

Lastly, she pulled off the cover of her bracelet and hesitated before snapping off the signal. It was the only way. Marc wasn't likely to be able to track her by it anyway. She swung her backpack on her shoulder and tested her luck. She headed into the hangar and went straight to the nearest security sign-in station.

The officers didn't even blink. Her card went through without a problem. Her story that she was a new soldier from the nearest moon of Paltka, filling in for his older brother on sick leave, passed the test when lightly checked on the basis that a military ship recently arrived from Paltka. She could now put her override device to the test.

Samantha stopped to grab the usual survival kit with its space blanket, communications device, pistol, three-month supply of edibles, and an unusual assortment of other items. She saw a handful of soldiers heading towards the aerospeeders, locked in their terminals on the lowest terrace. She followed them, lengthening her stride to match theirs. The captain glanced back and smiled at her.

"Hey! You're new here, aren't you? This must be your first patrol." Samantha nodded.

"I thought it might be interesting, so I figured I'd come along. I'm not sure what I'm supposed to do, though." The man laughed and glanced around before replying.

"You're a bit of a rascal, aren't you? Technically newbies shouldn't be coming unless it's assigned, but I'll let it fly this time. You can tag along with me and I'll show you what we do."

Samantha muttered under her breath, realizing that she may well be trapped, but she only expressed her thanks. The ID card unlocked the aerospeeder as the other men swung on. She didn't have a key for the bike. Samantha slipped the override device from her pocket and locked it in place under the dashboard. A turn of the dial brought an exhale of relief when the dashboard screens flashed on. She dumped her bag into the carrying compartment and mounted.

Her newfound friend flashed her a grin and they kicked their rides into gear, roaring out of the hangar. After the initial start-up, the aerospeeder was surprisingly a quiet, smooth ride. It glided swiftly at a cruising height of a few feet, but some of the men played around with its speed and aerobatics at a hundred feet.

When they hit the junction of the seven roads before the city, they split up. The captain waved Samantha after him and they veered off down one of the southern roads. The setting sun flashed red and yellow over the plains as they raced for the checkpoint high on a grassy hill. The captain dismounted and activated the station's systems.

"Now we watch," he said, "until, and if, the system picks up anything of interest."

"Such as?"

"Oh, the odd traveler, unauthorized vehicles, sand monsters, raid parties—"

"Not to seem naïve, but I haven't been here long. Raiding parties from where?" The captain laughed.

"Right, you're not from these parts. You may know that the King has been terrorizing several lesser kingdoms lately. A group of rebels, who call themselves the *Realtra*, have been pushing their luck and fighting back, whether by liberating slaves, burning a ship, or taking our supplies. We're not sure where they came from or where they hide, but we think they're from one or more of those kingdoms – Antiqua, Talorn, and Kedras specifically – and that they've found a home base down south somewhere, considering that they're often seen wearing heavy winter gear."

"I see," said Samantha, heart beating faster. If she could get away, would these rebels help her? She paced the hilltop.

By now, the sun had set. How long would it be before her vanishing act was discovered? If she left the station the captain would notify the other men; if she stunned him, she'd only have an hour.

The captain seemed to be spending most of his time watching her rather than the countryside. Samantha grew too lost in thought and too intent on scanning the hilltops and the systems for any sign of movement to notice the expression on his face. He finally walked over and grabbed her shoulder, causing her to jump. Turning her around, he scrutinized her face.

"So," he said. "You're from Paltka. But you don't look anything like a Paltkar... you have Almedran features, kid. And I can think of just one Almedran who is smart enough to come up with an idea like this, and desperate enough to do it." He pulled her hat from her head, revealing the tightly wrapped braids. Samantha's heart sank but she bravely met his amused, almost sympathetic expression.

"Alright, my lady, I won't bother to ask any questions because I can guess all the answers. I understand why you'd want to escape, and I won't stop you. But I can't help you, either."

Suddenly the system's scanner emitted a rapidly repeated beep. The captain glanced at it and informed her of two sets of bio signs in opposite directions. They were probably sand monsters out for a hunt – they weren't dangerous unless they happened to be starving, as they often were.

"Take the southwest quadrant," he told her. "I won't tell you to come back afterwards. Good luck!" He kissed her hand and headed for the southeast.

Samantha couldn't believe her luck already. That the captain would be willing to help her that far - What an excuse! If it were a sand monster, she could discard her soon-to-be-traitorous uniform and let it be assumed that she – or he as they thought – had been devoured for dinner.

Samantha leapt onto her aerospeeder and shot off down into the dark plain. The screens and lights auto-switched to stealth mode and the windshield was marked with a map in red and green. Samantha followed the blinking icon on the scan. She must have crossed several miles of the plains – this at a hundred feet – before she saw a glimpse of a dark hulking shape shuffling slowly over the rock and sand below.

The scanner now identified the object as definitely being a sand monster and brightened the image so that she could see the almost faceless, mournful mass. She wisely chose not to disturb it and brought her craft down a thousand yards away to exchange outfits. She was just bundling up the uniform, having been wearing her traveling dress underneath, when she looked up and saw something on the edge of a high sand dune.

There are few things more terrifying than seeing a formless shape in the empty desert, coming straight for you and almost upon you in the dark, and to hear only the *wumph, wumph, wumph* of its shuffling feet. Samantha froze momentarily in the automatic instant of terror, then shrieked instinctively and hurled the bundle of clothing into its face, if it even had one. She scrambled desperately onto the speeder amid the creatures horrifying moan and tore off, climbing as high as she could make the craft go.

Her heart beat in her ears. She glanced at the screen which told her that the creature had stopped its pursuit, out of energy, no doubt. She caught her breath and kept the scanner working. She didn't dare take the craft lower than fifty feet but she was soon out of the sand monster's habitat.

It was now only seven o'clock and the stars were shining out from the clouds. The terrain below consisted of flat red clay and stone, with the occasional loose rock. She slowed her pace and her distraction in searching the map for a possible destination blinded her to the blinking icon rapidly moving towards her.

A gust of wind turned her head just in time and she saw in the bright starlight a speeder that was almost upon her, the carmine markings of the King on its front blades –

"How?" she cried, and kicked the craft to Mach 1, staying close to the ground. Medrhos chased her over the flats, gaining every second while Samantha struggled to handle the speed and not panic. Medrhos was herding her towards the east – A noise like a bursting glass and something exploded – Samantha's craft slowed crazily and she threw herself off. This narrowly saved her as the speeder came crashing down and tumbled end over end before exploding in a ball of fire. Samantha leapt to her feet but Medrhos had already dismounted. He stared at her almost wildly, but with his usual amusement.

"Medrhos! Are you *trying* to kill me?! I swear, you must have a seventh sense!" Samantha exclaimed in half-frightened frustration, swaying as she tried to regain her own sense of balance and direction. "How did you track me this time?"

"Certainly not, and it was hardly difficult," he drawled. "Not when the captain of my guard told me all about your escapade."

"Double-crosser," Samantha muttered.

"He could hardly dare to do otherwise," Medrhos said softly, advancing. "He knows the consequences of being disloyal to me. But he also shows admirable chivalry in giving you the possibility of escape, for which I commend him."

Samantha stepped backwards, reluctantly drawing that infamous dagger. Perhaps she could get around him and take his speeder. Not likely, but it was worth a shot.

"Samantha, I know you won't use that dagger... you're too gentle and fond of me for that," he teased. "Listen to me. You have no chance of finding the people of the *Realtra*. I doubt they would look for one who is to be their enemy's queen."

Samantha stumbled over a loose stone, still moving backwards, dagger still warily in hand.

Medrhos' stare was almost paralyzing as he moved steadily forward. Samantha met his gaze and didn't waver, trying to think of a way to get away without using her dagger.

The ground vanished beneath her feet – in a whirlwind move Medrhos painfully snatched her wrist, whipped her around and pinned her back against him, leaving her with a view of a cavernous sunken pool, swimming with swirling green luminescence.

"I have something to tell you," he breathed in her ear, standing near the edge with her in front of him. "Karthos moved up the wedding. . . to twelve hours from now. And now watch, for this is where Karthos will bring you if you disappoint him."

The pool surged and a mouth opened – a face like a ghost, now formless, now reptilian – it asked to be fed. Samantha gasped and jumped as it wailed and waited for her to fall into its mouth. Medrhos held her close and didn't let her fall.

"It is not an instant death. . . it can drag out for a lifetime. A few have been rescued before but. . . they *survive*, not *live*. You don't want that to happen to you. *I* don't want anything to happen to you." He pulled her away from the edge and released her.

"It's your choice. I can make the former easy for you, and once you're a Marauder and my wife, I can keep Karthos from hurting you."

"How? You can't even keep him from hurting *you*."

"Try me," he replied, and mounted his bike. Samantha stood, looking at him as the wind blew around her. She glanced down and experimentally kicked a large rock into the pool. A moment later it was vomited out as violently as though it were shot from a cannon, blanched white.

"Yep, bad idea," Samantha muttered as she watched it roll to a stop a thousand feet away. Medrhos was waiting. Why couldn't he just understand?

"Medrhos, I . . . can't go with you. I don't love you! You tore my life apart, or maybe that was Karthos through you, and you kidnapped me. I'm not going to do anything for you – not like that, anyway. Karthos doesn't need to know that you let me go. Please understand Medrhos, and be my friend as you were long ago," she whispered. "Please! I know you still have good in you even if you bury it. *Try*, Medrhos!" The King's eyes had narrowed but he didn't seem to be fighting her.

"No," he said slowly, finally looking away. "Karthos *doesn't* know. And he's not going to. Despite what he's done to both of us you've still been a friend. . ." She didn't see him slipping his gun from its holster., rolling the setting dial from vortex to shock.

"You may not love me, *ancilla*, but I need you." He fired and watched Samantha crumple to the ground, stunned by the burst of electricity. He picked her up and laid her across the seat so gently she would have been surprised.

"I'm sorry," he whispered very low, and snapped the aerospeeder to Mach 1. Somehow the stars seemed to shine softer now as they swiftly neared the warmly glowing city that could have been masquerading as one of those comforting cities lit for the holidays. Samantha was only beginning to come to when Medrhos hid his speeder in the forested edge of the garden.

Taking the girl in his arms, he slipped through the garden and climbed the high, pedestaled wall up to Samantha's balcony. He set her gently on her bed and smiled when Lyona came running from some dark corner. The cat rubbed her head against Medrhos' knee, then leapt onto the bed to look from one to the other. The King stroked the cat's head, then nudged her under Samantha's arm where she promptly fell asleep.

Samantha's eyes were halfway open; she was almost fully conscious but too worn out to bother stirring. Medrhos looked down at her for some time, all the harshness and worry fading from his face. He stooped over her.

"I wish, I wish, I wish, Samantha! That you knew. . ." He touched her dark hair very softly. Samantha felt a strange pang – that strange mix of sadness and comfort you can get all at once at Christmas. She wanted to take the chance to say something but she felt too paralyzed. Medrhos turned and quietly left the way he had come, shutting the balcony door behind him.

XII

Slated

When Samantha awoke the next morning, it was in the pitch-black of pre-dawn to the glow of the lights above her and the bustling of a dozen handmaids. Silvestra gently pulled Samantha out of bed and the engineer remembered what Medrhos had said. Her heart sank; she went cold and her head spun when she looked at the garments and ornaments laid out. She instinctively reached for the blessed medal Ransomme had given her on her last visit.

The image of the Holy Face was etched upon it and Samantha's fingers wandered over each feature. The wind blew as in an echo to her feelings when she stepped onto the balcony to wake herself up. She knelt and breathed a prayer. The handmaidens, while anxious due to the fact that the wedding would take place at dawn, waited patiently..

Moving the rosary beads through her fingers lowered Samantha's stress until, fully awake, she began to seek a way out of her predicament. Either she could attempt what was likely another futile escape, or she could try to find a way out of the wedding.

She sighed and felt a headache coming on as she wondered why she hadn't fought Medrhos more forcibly from the beginning. Then again, the fact that she had fought with sarcasm and conquered each challenge he threw at her seemed to only make him like her more. She had done everything she could have.

This realization brought a touch of healing. For the first time since the Marauders' had made their mark on her, Samantha felt a flicker of freedom and hope, and the stars no longer shone with a sad coldness, but danced with joy as God had made them to do. For there is no joy or freedom but His.

Samantha turned and looked at the wedding garments and the sweet, worried faces of her handmaids. She rushed to embrace them.

"Don't worry, I'll tell Medrhos I'll be late."

She picked up her watch and signaled him, briefly explaining that she was running behind. The cold, dull fear was setting in again quickly, but that was normal. Everything was always temporary.

She put on the sharply cut sweeping dress of obsidian and amaranth. It was customary for Marauder weddings, though Medrhos had made an allowance for the Almedran silver-white waterfall gown to be worn during the celebration the following day.

Two of the handmaids gathered Samantha's hair, weaving it with raven extensions and golden ornaments, looping and coiling it around the back of her head until it felt like a weight, drawing her head back to keep her posture perfect. Earrings, a few chains and gems were added, and then came the massive, heavy metal crown. It looked like a fantastic piece of metallic coral with its rows of paper thin, slender spikes dotted with smothered gems and bloody rubies.

Samantha looked at it with distaste as two of the girls fitted it high on her brow. It curved around in the back, neatly matching the coils of her hair. It must have weighed ten pounds at least! Standing tall would have been impossible if not for the corseted dress and the heeled boots that paired with her outfit. She looked like an alien tyrant queen if there ever was one. She stared at her reflection.

Ten years ago, she never would have imagined this. Eight years ago, it became her worst nightmare. For the following eight years it had vaguely haunted her like a legendary curse from the pages of a dusty tome. Now, it was reality as though she had stepped into a mirror and was looking back at the girl who had been, the woman who should have been, and the future that had seemed so near and safe with Marc, Aiyra, and Konstan. Now the first mirror had been blackened and the last two shattered, leaving her staring at the pane of glass in which she stood.

"Through a mirror darkly. . ."

The world seemed to grow vast before her eyes until the stars and worlds blotted themselves out with their numbers and she stood cold in a space that was neither black nor white. She saw each world spinning, not randomly like a child's top set to play but with a precision that was dancelike.

She looked down and she saw nations working with each other, for each other, against each other. She looked closer still and there she saw man, woman, and child all holding close in the way they thought was best, some blind while others not, all fighting for what they thought they and others needed, and never knowing when they walked the path set before them, never seeing the angels that pulled them back on track.

It came down to this, then, that the world consisted only of one thing, family, instinctively reaching for what each thought was love and goodness and safety, and that each human soul had a purpose whether it saw it or not, whether it fulfilled it or not, whether it failed. The very planets, the stars, the streams, fountains, fires and floods moved at the spoken Word, set in motion when God planned the world's greatest play with the cast He loved most.

The world shrank again and found Samantha looking into the mirror. The masks she had made for herself which she had never known now fell away, leaving before her eyes the carefree, gentle-hearted girl who now possessed such strengths, abilities, and love that she never would have imagined.

Fear and fire fell away. She had seen the world and its people and she knew them. She knew Medrhos, and even Karthos. More importantly, she knew the God Who loved more than the world and its heavens could hold, more than man can hate himself, more than it takes to lift the world's greatest villain and say 'I forgive you.'

She saw the smile and heard the laugh that no man ever hears in this life, a child, a man's, and the voice deep in the earth itself, all at once – the one in the falling of cherry blossoms, the dance of the fire, the rush of the wind with its tender kiss, the crashing of the waves, the singing brook and shining moon. In every hour of darkness and misery that laugh could be heard because He alone knew the final act; it was the closest He gave man to reading ahead. Samantha laughed, for even Lyona's purr and sudden antics voiced this laugh. She turned to her handmaids and smiled.

"Quickly, quickly!" she said merrily. "I mustn't miss my own wedding! It's a game two must play at."

The cat meowed in reply and gave a laugh-like yawn. Bewildered, Silvestra hastily hung the heavy Almedran mantle over Samantha's shoulders and the other handmaids either took hold of the train or held the door.

The sky was turning to a sweet violet haze with a faint band of gold on the horizon when Samantha stepped out into the chill of the winged courtyard, looking over the garden with the city far below to their left. Medrhos' men lined the long walkway, all in leather and gold, looking silently, protectively at the one who was so out of place in Marauder colors as she passed through their ranks. On the far end a makeshift altar had been erected, guarded by two fire basins of jade and jasper; the fire was warm and friendly as Ransomme, Medrhos, and Karthos stood before it. Samantha walked slowly, studying their faces.

Ransomme, in his black cassock and white robe (he had no vestments which he could wear for they had been left on the *Delta*) looked worn but his eyes were reassuring. Karthos stood all in darkest navy and gray with his silver beard drawn to a point, his braided mane drifting in the breeze. He was almost threatening, yet somehow Samantha could feel that proud grandfatherly spark when he looked at her. She wondered, could she draw it out of him? Yes, but not yet. She turned her eyes on the man she was currently slated to wed.

He was clothed in the same colors as she, with heavy mantle and gloves banded with gold with a ruby gem bound in the center of the back of his hand. She looked into his face, fear nearly returning. Karthos or no Karthos, Medrhos had too much cruelty and wrath within him to be safe. In his eyes flashed pride, both good and bad, and yet there was something else in his face that made her hold her tongue and wait and watch. Coran stepped forward, took her mantle, and cast it on the ground.

"Samantha Mariel Anselle," Medrhos said sharply, loud enough for all his men to hear, towering over her on the steps before the altar. "You have the gifts needed to belong with us as a Marauder. It has been granted to you to become one of us. But for that gift you must pay the price."

What gift? Samantha thought, as Medrhos motioned for her to drop to the ground. Two of Medrhos' men slowly moved from the walls and strode in a half circle, stopping behind her. Each held a torch they had lit in the flames. Karthos raised his head and his hands, cloak billowing around him, and shouted in a strange language – the ancient Marauder tongue now kept alive only in such ceremonies.

"*Kalidemm ta'mizirjat kani-darr!*"

"*Varadan, kanimar kani alve vani kayal kirkal ugratal....*" The two men behind Samantha began chanting in a low drone, eyes fixed on Medrhos. Samantha's brain swirled with confusion as she thought the sky went dark again, gray with clouds and wind as the torches burned darker. But then the sky was only the lightening gray of dawn as the ranks of men slowly took up the chant until it swelled and rang off the stones and abruptly stopped, leaving the air and Samantha's ears ringing.

"*Iridhas.*" Medrhos spoke this last word as though it were an amen – but he didn't seem to be fully present. He opened his eyes again and looked straight at Samantha.

"Samantha Mariel Anselle, the people you call your own are yours no longer. You chose to take our challenges and you passed them; your loyalty belongs to us now. Do you swear it?"

Could she? She had to.

"My blood will be as of your blood, your people shall be my people, your laws my laws; the heart of your kin shall be as mine."

Medrhos' jaw dropped for a split-second. This wasn't the Samantha he knew. Almedrans took such words seriously. He carried on.

"So be it." He loosened his gauntlet. Pulling the ceremonial knife from its sheath he cut his own arm and held it over one of the fires until the dripping blood began to burn. She hadn't thought the blood part would be in any way literal. She winced.

Medrhos stepped forward and pressed his wrist against Samantha's brow. She sucked her breath in with a gasp as the scar burned again and with a pained look, Medrhos grabbed her right hand in his left, keeping his other held to her scar.

"*Varrani kin id-dar, zar-demm ta'var valix,*" he intoned. There was a pause. "Yes, you're supposed to repeat it," he hissed. Samantha looked to Ransomme who just nodded and she obeyed. After a long string of these strange chants Medrhos released her. The scar on her brow was red with his blood but clean as an engraving. He stepped back and looked at her.

"Tabitha Maeris Ancilla, my people bid you welcome, as do I."

Tabitha – it was almost Talitha. Could he have done that on purpose? He certainly did know of Talitha's death since he had sent Marc back to her. . . Samantha wondered as Medrhos removed his own mantle now, draping it over her shoulders in a sign of the king's protection. He lifted to her feet and the men abruptly started chanting her new name like happy young boys might when their favorite sports player scores a goal. Medrhos allowed himself one shadow of a proud smile and took Samantha up to the altar. Now it was his turn to kneel.

Samantha was mildly surprised that her head wasn't spinning. She felt a bit out of it yet everything was clear; the sun was beginning to peek over the horizon as Ransomme began to pray the Mass. Samantha was confused; wasn't he supposed to begin with the wedding vows?

Samantha thought that based on her current state she wouldn't even be strained when that moment came but when Ransomme finished his all too brief sermon (Marauder patience was at stake and he couldn't count on anyone but Samantha to listen anyway), her heart abruptly began to pound. Medrhos stood and she followed suit. Was she awake or dreaming?

Now Ransomme was turning towards them and her heart pounded in her ears. She must have been pale but she forced herself to calm down, pay attention, and not think. That would have been the most stressful thing she could have done right then. An *Ave* ran on repeat through her mind instead.

"Since it is your intention to marry, join your right hands and declare your consent before God," Ransomme was saying. Medrhos took her hand firmly in his.

"I, Medrhos, Marauder, King, and Empire's Heir, take you, Ancilla, to be my wife. I vow to be true to you even if I lose my throne or my life. I will love you and protect you until my death or yours." He looked squarely into her eyes, gripping her hand tightly. Ransomme turned to her.

"Samantha, will you vow the same?"

Samantha stared. Several things were already messed up in this ceremony – and wasn't she supposed to repeat the entire vow – but that was the wrong set of words. What was going on? She saw Medrhos look to Ransomme in the bride's moment of confusion, and the priest nodded imperceptibly as Samantha opened her mouth to speak. She didn't get one word out before Medrhos pulled her into his arms and held her tight as the sun rose and lit them both. Karthos turned to Ransomme.

"Aren't you supposed to say 'man and wife?" he demanded.

"Man and wife?" Ransomme repeated innocently.

Medrhos released Samantha then, whose head was definitely spinning now as Karthos took the crown from her head and replaced it with the Queen's diadem. They knelt again as Ransomme carried on with the Mass. The Eucharist cleared Samantha's mind as she tried to pray. That glance and nod between Medrhos and Ransomme could only mean that the discrepancies in the ceremony were on purpose. *They weren't married!* And Karthos was none the wiser.

The moment Mass was ended, Medrhos pulled Samantha to her feet and took her down amongst his men, who came shyly to offer her a kiss. She didn't know that all of them knew the secret, for Medrhos trusted his men both with his life and his bride.

"Go and rest now, Ancilla," he said, walking her inside. "Our wedding supper will be, unfortunately, with Karthos, so that we may prepare you. Tomorrow we shall present you to my - *our* - people."

"Medrhos, why?!" Samantha broke out, surprising herself. After all that Medrhos had done, how had he come to the decision to not marry her?

"Why with Karthos or why tomorrow? Because you wanted a second dress."

"No! You know what I'm asking – you left out half the wedding and I *know* you know that."

Medrhos gave her an amused smile and he pulled her along. "I thought you'd be happy, Ancilla. I'm not ready to marry you yet; Karthos has a knack for rushing things, doesn't he? We'll marry in secret in eight months' time. This way, you get a reprieve, Karthos is pleased, and I get the full powers of an empire." He clenched one fist with a satisfied smile and squeezed her hand, stopping in front of her room. Samantha turned to him.

"Oh yes, he has a knack for rushing things. And you have a knack for acquiring bonuses for yourself! You win on all accounts," she said almost angrily. "And what happens when Karthos demands to meet Medrhos junior?" Clearly Medrhos had not thought that through and he looked like someone who just had their head nearly cut off.

"Uh. . . well, there are plenty of children in the slave orphanage. I'm sure you'd be happy to adopt one. Or two. That's kind of in your line of work as queen, so do what you want. And hurry up and get ready, will you?" He rushed off.

Samantha shook her head in mild frustration. Well, at least she wasn't married. It was God's Will that she be free for now and improve her acting skills. She'd be in the limelight soon enough in Scene I, the irrelevant reception with very little to celebrate. But first the introit.

XIII

Bound

The late afternoon found Medrhos, Karthos, and Samantha seated around a lengthy triangular table draped with golden-white lace and dripping with flowers. They had left the dining hall for a cliff-side sunroom, where the light poured in among the tapestries and guarding fountains that soothed Samantha's nerves.

The three watched silently as servers ladened the table with steaming tureens of soup, cornucopias of sun-kissed grapes, and platters of foreign meats. Heavy meat tarts were side by side with stuffed chicken breast with goat cheese and potatoes, vinegar salad with onions and sliced beef, and meatballs laden with cream sauce. Chalices of iced wine with lemonberries were set before them and dishes of marinated mushrooms, olives, and parsley were there to add flavor to anything deemed even a tad tasteless.

Samantha surveyed the table. What was with all the meat? Not a familiar dish in sight, nor one that seemed particularly palatable at the moment. It would seem that Karthos had banned Almedran food from the dinner table now that Samantha had become Maeris. That was her official name, Tabitha being an extraneous name and Ancilla an epithet. But neither of the men cared to use anything but Ancilla as yet. Karthos helped himself to a large portion of meat and mushrooms, crusty bread with balsamic, and potatoes as soon as the servants had left them.

"Now that we have all that over with," he announced, passing the platter to an annoyed Medrhos, "have you thought about what I asked you?"

Medrhos made a point of pushing the tray to Samantha so she could serve herself before he did. She took only the bread and the mushrooms.

"My answer is the same."

"I see. It's very unlike you, but then again, you *may* only get married once in your life," Karthos said dryly. "Your father had several wives, you know."

"Don't be disgusting," Medrhos returned. His eyes turned to Samantha, who, if she weren't busy staring at the table, would have been wearing an appalled expression. Samantha pushed the tray back to Medrhos, eyeing the length of the table and wondering why she was so far away from him when she was close to Karthos. She would have felt a *little* safer from Karthos if she were closer to Medrhos. Glancing up, she redirected the conversation, noting the sparks flying between both men's eyes.

"Is it tradition for a Queen to have enough room for a river to run between her and the King?" she asked innocently. "Or can I move." They stopped and looked at her. Medrhos waved his hand.

"Whatever," he sighed, but looked less uptight, and rather pleased when Samantha set her chair beside him. Karthos forced himself to acknowledge Samantha's presence and turned to a different subject.

"So," he said, cutting his great slab of unidentifiable meat. "I've been hearing tales of these pesky rebels from down south. On top of Kadmos and Cajetan, their princes, they seem to have suddenly acquired a leader who is too smart for our soldiers. Excuse me, *your* soldiers, of course. I've heard the man called Orion; he seems uncatchable and it's rubbing off on the rest of those rebels. Have any ideas on how to deal with them?"

"Plenty," Medrhos replied icily over his wine.

"Such as?"

Medrhos gave his grandfather a patronizingly patient look of annoyance. "I don't discuss war and weddings in the same breath. What did they teach you when you were a kid? *Anything*?"

Startled, Samantha choked on a laugh and hastily popped a grape into her mouth. Karthos glared at her and returned the condescending smile of his grandson.

"Oh, you'd be surprised. They taught me everything I taught you." He trained his eyes on Samantha. He knew just how to repay her for that laugh. With that, he launched into his favorite subject: his training of Medrhos.

The look on the King's face would have been hilarious in any other circumstance, but his embarrassment and discomfort were for a good reason - the tales were horrendous. Karthos was evil, and Medrhos was bad, but Samantha had never imagined that Karthos could have led Medrhos to do the things he now documented.

The stories of Medrhos' acts of revenge against his enemies mingled with what Karthos thought to be 'good education' - terrorism. Unimaginable deaths, sickening slavery, unspeakable torture, insane punishments, bizarre one-sided treaties, pillaging and raids, the blood on his hands - Samantha felt sick and she felt the blood drain from her face, leaving her lightheaded. According to these words, Medrhos was a murderer. Karthos, laughing, turned to her and warned her to watch her own life.

Medrhos was furious that Karthos found all this an amusing way of entertaining and terrorizing the young queen. His hand gripped the knife by his plate but found Samantha's hand there instead.

Startled, he gave her a tender look and a timid smile that asked if she would be alright. Samantha could never have smiled back, but she squeezed his hand before letting go and slid the knife off the table lest temptation strike. She had had more than enough, and so had he.

"Karthos, stop." She was still white-faced and was surprised to find that her voice was level. Karthos tightened his lips and looked at the engineer who had dared tell him to be silent.

"I don't know if it's a tradition to tell a bride every sin on her husband's soul, but that's no way to celebrate a wedding."

The man silently downed his wine, eyes fixed on her.

"It's a pity," he said slowly, rubbing the engraved rim of his glass, "that we didn't have you pass the same test as we Marauders always go through. It would have put you in your place long before now and I'd have a much better granddaughter to show for it. But then again you wouldn't be you if you had your will taken from you, would you?"

"I'm still a Christian," Samantha replied, gripping Medrhos' hand hard to keep him from speaking. "Currently that's not a crime, as evidenced by the fact that you had our wedding follow that tradition. It's how I live and why I speak. You ought to know already that I don't believe in giving myself into anyone's power save for the One I believe in. So, if you aren't satisfied with me and you think every young woman should be subjected to mental torture and made to hate the man she just married, I suggest you find a different way of testing my loyalty."

The man only laughed in reply. "You speak as I expected, my dear. Even though you are a Christian and must be tamed, I'm still proud of you." He turned to Medrhos. "Have it done. She must be tested again."

The King's eyes narrowed. "No."

"Medrhos."

"I won't do that to Ancilla! She already passed the tests and came through fire, and she's a quick learner: quick enough without having her force-fed everything you say."

"Medrhos, it needs to be done. If you don't, the cult is prepared to propose a new king for your queen and a new bride for you. I'm only their ambassador to you. That's not my desire, but I have been warned. Even with her gifts, they want to be sure she is 'safe.'"

Medrhos leaned back in his chair. "Guess what. All that would bother me for about two and a half minutes before I conveniently find a few new statues for my great hall."

Karthos nearly spat out his wine. "You fool, you know you can't utilize your new powers until they've authorized your reign in person, and that only when you've instigated your Great Raid!"

"I'd do it to you and to them if any of you so much as imply one more thing about her," Medrhos snarled. "You're lucky I haven't done it yet!"

Karthos put down his goblet and tried to pacify him. "Easy, son, you'll have plenty of time to punish me later. I don't *want* this done to Ancilla, but for her sake and yours I hope you do it and satisfy them. It would be a very unlucky time to lose the favor of the cult."

"I don't care if-"

"I'm sorry to interrupt your fascinating conversation," Samantha interjected, putting down her fork. She had finally managed to stay the lightheaded feeling and had been trying to eat, though that hadn't been working well. "Since I seem to be the one discussed, could you explain exactly what you're talking about? Precisely, what powers are we talking about?"

Medrhos let out his breath. "As you know, Ancilla, kings pass from mere warrior to king, and then to emperor through strategic marriage. Before today, I was only a king, with the powers of my warriors alone; the rest was managed through the governing of our senate, which I, of course, was a major participant in. But now I govern myself fully and have the power to move that empire which is mine. I can destroy or save whatsoever I wish." He eyed Karthos. "I'm afraid you will be seeing an example soon enough, Ancilla."

"Aaand can we clarify this cult?"

"Descendants of the original Marauders, radicals, et cetera," Medrhos muttered. "They make the rules and we mostly don't listen to 'em." He leaned over and looked at her plate, which she had hardly touched. "I'm sorry, Ancilla, that he had to ruin your appetite. I'll see to it that when you feel better something is made for you."

"Hm. Alright, fascinating. And thank you, Medrhos. I hope there's a wedding cake on this menu," Samantha sighed, staring at the table full of meat. "Women can't survive on meat alone, you know, that's what you men seem to do."

Both men were amused and the conversation turned to lighter things, but left each with dark thoughts.

~~~

The following day. . .

Medrhos stepped out onto the great balcony overlooking the city. The bedecked streets glistened in the morning light and were flooded with his people. He didn't speak, only stepped aside and drew Samantha forward. The warmth of the greeting given by those below shocked her for the second time. But more than that she could scarcely believe that half the throng were clearly not Marauders. They were Almedran! Medrhos was smiling. He had spoken the truth when he had said that he had saved her people.

"You should learn to trust me, Ancilla," he said softly to her. "*Sometimes.*" He grinned and pulled her back when she moved to go down among her people. "Karthos will be angry. . . you're one of us now, Ancilla, remember that."

He nodded to one of his captains, who opened the gates to the palace hall. Almedrans and Marauders alike poured in as the King led his bride to her seat at his side on the raised dais. Before the instruments and wine glasses could be broken out, Karthos faced the gathering and held up his hand. Of course, he *had* to make a speech. Medrhos rolled his eyes at Samantha, who, in her strained state, had to bite her tongue to avoid laughing.

"Our brethren and dear friends, we've all waited years for the Empire to regain its king. King Eudorius fell nearly twenty years ago warring against our enemies, putting our economy and his people first. Since then our Empire has not been the same, nor as stable or as well-friended as under his rule, and he left no son to fill his place. We needed a King who would not falter before our enemies or anything in this short life, one who could guard even the children of those in our Empire whom he knows least."

"My friends, you chose me to discover and to create the heir to the throne as is our age-old custom in such times. And there was only one who was worthy to become that heir: my own grandson. I say this not out of pride, for you know my calling led me to reject even my own family; but I never would have chosen him. It was a Voice that led me to choose him. He alone could fulfill our needs and the requirements of a king. We all watched as he passed the tests that no ordinary man could survive, nor resist failure. You watched him become your Guardian, your Warrior, your Lord, and then your King. And now, today, by the gift of a bride who gives him her own world, he has become your Emperor."

Samantha suddenly felt sick and very worried. Her world – *her own world?* Almedra was gone, what was left but Vestar – and all of its territories! Medrhos dropped his hand on hers, resting on the arm of her throne.

"Remember what you overheard him say in the armory," he hissed softly. "He's only projecting now and could find a thousand other reasons to call me an emperor. No doubt he will make a speech of every one of them before noon!"

Samantha drew a deep breath and gave him a grateful glance as Karthos proposed a toast. Then came the endless procession of men and their wives coming to humbly greet and congratulate the king and his bride. One young mother came shyly up to Samantha, clothed in an Almedran working dress and shawl, embroidered with forest flowers.

"Please forgive me for coming like this," she apologized. "I can only stay a little while. . . I just wanted you to know that we won't forget that you are one of us, miss, and we can only imagine all that you have been through-" she glanced at Medrhos. The sleeping child on her back mumbled softly in his sleep. The woman looked back at Samantha, who was half-confused.

"It's a hard calling that only *you* can do. But there are thousands who will help you. We believe in you. Like me, you are a mother – a mother of thousands, of rich and poor, young and old. Your heart alone was made for caring for them as few Queens could; yet you and I are of the same blood." She looked affectionately at Samantha and impulsively kissed her. "Be brave, sweet, and don't fear. The God Who loves you will never leave you alone. No one who has ever loved you will abandon you."

She lifted her head a little with a knowing smile and suddenly Samantha was reminded of the man who had spoken to her in the compound. The words didn't quite add up, coming from one of her subjects and fellow Almedrans. She watched the woman vanish into the crowd and turned to Medrhos.

His expression was reminiscent of one who had been sucking on an excessively sour lemon. Perhaps that was due to Karthos beginning another speech for anyone who would listen. Medrhos motioned for the music to be played louder and his grandfather's voice was soon drowned out with the help of a few glasses of wine.

Lords and ladies, soldiers and citizens, and cruel emissaries whose voices and temperament chilled Samantha through, all came before her with gifts great, small, tasteless, and tactful. She skeptically eyed a basket of smelly fish beside an ivory box laden with gems carved like roses.

Medrhos himself had gifted her a tiger, a breed of the Arrenian and Almedran strains; it sat beside her throne docilely, great golden eyes studying the crowd when it wasn't eyeing the basket of fish. Medrhos had already named it for her: Silmä, the ancient word for Tiger's-eye, hence the matching bejeweled collar around the cat's neck.

Medrhos seemed quite fond, and altogether synonymous with the creature, Samantha noted, as she reached down and ruffled her new pet's ears. That day, to match her foregoing of the traditional attire in favor of Almedra, he had taken the tiger's colors for his own.

Gelert didn't seem to trust the newcomer yet; he was bent equally upon guarding the basket of fish as he was his mistress, until Samantha laughed and fed one to each, for even Gelert had a taste for the sea. She dismissed them for play, and soon both animals were engaged in a game of hide and seek spanning the entirety of the hall. She turned back to the gift givers.

A slave trader bowed and flung a slave at her feet. Angered, Samantha slapped him and ordered the child's chains removed.

"Silvestra, take her to my room and see to it that she gets food and rest," she said aside. The amazed look given her by the child and the embrace that followed made Samantha want to weep. She knelt and held her close.

"What's your name, little one?"

"Estill, ma'am."

"Well, consider yourself adopted, Estill," Samantha said softly.

Medrhos glanced sharply at her, in the midst of his diplomatic conversation with the king of a well-known tuna company. Whatever his thoughts at the sudden proposed fatherhood, he was soon swept away into Karthos' circle of dignitaries and Samantha was left alone on the dais as the never-ending line finally began to thin out.

Two men were her last well-wishers. The first was tall, wrapped in an indigo cloak, and his foreign costume dictated that she could not see his face. The only thing that stood out to her was the ornate clasp on his shoulder, of three suns bound in a diamond frame It seemed to be a crest of sorts, but not one she recognized. It certainly was not of Marauder craftsmanship. The man stood half a moment, looking at the Queen who was sizing him up. Somehow she knew he was smiling. He dropped to kiss her hand without a word. With a bow, he left her.

Samantha distinctly felt that he alone, in that crowd of hundreds, had truly adopted her as his queen. This even though he was a foreigner! And somehow she knew that it was not because she was the queen of the empire, for this man, she was sure, was not an upholder of slavery. What kind of man was he? Her musings were interrupted.

A young foreigner trekked up the stairs, a soldier of some kind judging by the stiff, tarnished silver uniform he wore. He bowed with a flourish of his segmented cape, reminding Samantha of the near-dead tales of fanged men in the mountains of northern Almedra.

"O my fair Queen..."

"Get to the point," she said lightly. "I'm sure I have your speech memorized."

"Very well," he smiled, and came closer, an object glinting in his hand. Something didn't feel right. Samantha pushed him away, stepping backwards as the expression on the man's face became far more intent.

"My lady, it's only a gift!" he insisted. He lifted a glittering silver coronet as though to place it on her brow. Samantha resisted and glanced about for a means of retreat. Well, now those smelly fish could come in handy. She kicked the basket over.

Fish slid everywhere and down the stairs into the guests and the soldier nearly slipped. He caught himself and snatched Samantha's arm as the guests below jumped. Samantha stumbled and her back slammed against the edge of the arm of her throne, stunning her. Medrhos struggled through the crowd. He didn't make it to the dais before Samantha's cry cut through the lively music. The King glimpsed the girl's hands flying to her head and saw her collapse as the soldier stood there.

A second later the offender found himself flying through the air as Medrhos kicked the fish out of the way and him with it. Samantha was lying very still - Medrhos dropped down and gathered her up. The sight of the coronet turned his heart cold.

"No, no, no," he breathed and touched her white cheek with his still-gloved hand. She stirred and looked tremblingly into his eyes.

"Please take it off," she whispered. The bare white and iris crystal was digging into her brow and her strength, and very nearly her will, had been sucked from her. Medrhos stared. He had never seen Samantha broken. He had never seen her in the role of the sweet, frightened child, even on Almedra.

A Samantha who could not shield herself! A Samantha who needed protection! A Samantha who needed him, who begged for him to be her friend.

Samantha was too busy fighting that same power, again trying to bend her to its will, nearly numbing her, to notice. It blocked her thoughts and she could scarcely control her own movements, and when she tried, her nerves tingled and forced her to lie still.

A Samantha without her will was not Samantha, yet the most dreadful law which no Marauder dares to break bound him not to touch that crown. Medrhos felt his heart being wrenched in a dozen directions. Comfort her, he could, but he couldn't help her.

"There's nothing I can do for you, Ancilla," he replied. "It is forbidden." He looked at his grandfather. "You did this," he snarled, just low enough to keep onlookers from hearing. "You wanted it done! How much did you pay him?"

"I didn't and no, not like this," Karthos muttered. "She'll have to wear it for at least twenty-four hours. Unless, of course, she manages to destroy it," he said dryly. Aside, he told the guests to return to their own business.

Unsatisfied, Medrhos looked down at Samantha. No matter whether he wished her to love him and obey him, for twenty-four hours the Samantha he knew might cease to exist unless somehow she could destroy the crystal just as she had destroyed the basin. There was nothing he could do – unless he was willing to risk rebelling against that most grave command, the violation of which could cost him everything.

XIV

Possession

Not giving in was torture. It was as excruciating as trying to take just one more step in a blizzard to avoid freezing to death, or trying not to think of water in a desert with nothing but sand for a hundred miles in any direction. Trying to think of lasting twenty-four hours was even worse.

And yet when Medrhos spoke, she had to listen. He was the only one who could help her. He had asked her to trust him – sometimes. She guessed this would have to be one of those 'sometimes.' He ordered her to follow him, leaving the guests to continue the banquet.

Medrhos opened the door to Samantha's room and ordered Silvestra to make her comfortable and to keep young Estill out of the way. He stood in silence and watched as the handmaids dimmed the lights, made a fire, pulled back the covers, and programmed the windows to dim the afternoon light. His hands restlessly clenched and unclenched repeatedly.

Samantha stood in the middle of the room, unseeing, fighting the numbness that bound her. At least she was fighting. This time an *Ave* wasn't going to do the trick. She'd either go down, or last until she was freed twenty-four hours later.

"Samantha, rest," said Medrhos. His voice, though strained, was reassuring.

It was alright to listen to him. Marc, Ransomme, her parents all would have told her to do the same. She let herself drop onto the bed. Medrhos stood at the bedside for some time, killing himself for not tearing the band off Samantha's brow. He took a deep breath and smiled grimly.

"I may be forbidden to help you, Ancilla, but I'm not forbidden to punish the man who did this to you! And if I find that Karthos lied to me. . . he will die." He stooped and kissed the girl who was not at all soothed by that or his words, and left her in the dark.

It soon became evident to Silvestra and the other handmaids, who sat silently in the parlor, that Medrhos' command to rest had not been a wise one, though natural. They all had assumed that since the will was effectively at rest during sleep, the crystal's effect would also sleep. Instead it introduced the strangest dreams to Samantha's brain, so real she felt entirely conscious.

It tried to shape her personality in her sleep, building on what Karthos and Medrhos had done to her. It showed her what she would be as a Marauder, and made her feel like she *was* one. She was sharing in Medrhos' reign, but she was even more terrible than he, for cruelty in a woman is far more unnatural than in a man.

Her heart was like ice as she guided Medrhos' hand in subduing slaves and kingdoms. Her deceptions smashed Vestar, which was all too willing to believe her word. She laughed at Karthos' terrorism and tripled it.

All the while she was shuddering inside, feeling out of place with those horrible emotions and actions.

There was a wedding ring bound on her finger, and she showed it to Marc, who was in chains, and the expression would have torn Samantha's heart, but not Queen Maeris'. She wasn't Ancilla anymore, but a queen with the web-weaving skill of a spider. Even Medrhos, who loved her, fell into her traps more than once.

Her engineering skills were used in training a corps to create and utilize weapons of mass torture which would render dozens defenseless at once, increasing the ranks of the slaves quicker than ever.

And she saw Marc again and taunted him with memories of Talitha, and punished him for his attempts to destroy Medrhos' – no, *her* – empire.

The pain in his eyes shocked Samantha within Maeris awake and she began to fight. This was a dream; it *had* to be. She would never do this to Marc!

Her head began to hurt and she remembered the band upon her brow. It tried to numb her and Maeris tried to stifle her. If she couldn't pray, how could she resist? She felt herself weakening and began to panic.

I don't believe in giving myself into anyone's power save for the One I believe in. . . . Samantha heard her own words again. That was the key. The numbness hesitated. Her prayer echoed again.

Ransomer, I'll be a slave one way or another. . . . If I must be one, let me be Yours! She felt peace creeping in amidst her anxious thoughts.

I will Your Will alone. Take mine! The crystal flashed on her brow. It spat sparks through her nerves – she was holding her own but it seemed God thought it best not to save her, only to aid her with His strength.

The crystal struggled with her mentally. Images flashed through her mind of the glowing cavern with its walls of hexagonal crystals, then, a heavy chain around a man's neck engraved with a bird of prey.

Blood, blood, blood, and fire! Samantha's mind was burning and she wanted to scream, if she had even known how, and if she had been in control of her own mouth. She had to survive–

Fiery wings, shadows, a laughing skull and an indescribably horrible face that could have been a skeletal dragon's head - despair and anger mingled with laughter and pain. *Give in!*

Samantha shook her head. She had to keep fighting. It was getting harder and more painful with each passing moment. She was so out of it now that the images were to her a whirlwind of red and blue. It was all she could do to lock herself up in a corner of her mind to resist.

Why, oh why! Where was Medrhos when she needed him? Always there when she didn't want him, always helping when she didn't desire it, always seeming to know her thoughts except now that her thoughts were scarcely her own. She was standing on a high wall now, a dark burning forest before her feet.

What was this torture? How could she last a day, even another minute? What fiend had invented this – *Don't jump, no don't jump* -

An icy fire suddenly ripped through her body and then she went numb. The images and sounds ceased with a jerk. Something snapped and it was as though she had suddenly broken through the lake ice after nearly drowning.

Her eyes flew open at the strangeness of the silence and the lack of pain, but she couldn't see so she closed them again. Her body felt damaged, as though it had been smashed against a cliff-face. Blood trickled down her face and wet her eyelashes. The crystal had drawn blood from her again.

The wind was whistling softly around her and it was dark out. Where was she? Someone had his arm around her shoulders, lifting her off the pavement. Her eyes finally focused.

"Medrhos," she whispered. He was kneeling beside her, the vermilion gems glowing like fire on his gloves. The smoking, twisted coronet was in his left hand, and as she watched, he clenched his fist. The now blood-red crystal exploded with a flash and the silver band melted away into dust.

"You. . . said you couldn't. . ." Samantha tried to fix her eyes on his face again. "Your powers. . . too. . ." Medrhos clenched his jaw and looked down at her.

"It was forbidden. But Karthos undermined the King, and the King does as he pleases. You were never to suffer this way. They promised they wouldn't touch you, Ancilla. Their lies are well repaid with scorn." He stooped and gently kissed the bleeding scar.

"They won't touch you again, Ancilla. I'll see to that." His eyes glinted in the dark. He gathered her up and carried her down from the castle wall. His arms were so strong and safe and his heart beat rhythmically in her ear. Her eyes fluttered shut. She was so exhausted she couldn't even murmur in reply.

~~~

Samantha, despite her exhaustion, found sleeping difficult. Her mind was filled with the disturbing images she had seen. The medallion kept flashing before her eyes. Why? And then it hit her.

She dragged herself out of bed. Silvestra started awake from the chair in which she had been keeping watch, and tried to restrain her mistress. She had hardly been in bed for a half hour yet -

"Medrhos," Samantha whispered dizzily. "Where is he?" Silvestra hesitated and then pointed out the window. Firelight glimmered deep in the forest. Samantha's heart sank.

"Karthos?"

Silvestra nodded. Then there was no time to lose. Samantha forced herself on her feet, shook the colored sparks out of her vision, and ran. She leapt down the ramparts and tore through the trees. She had never been in this area before, and her slippers sank in the mud. Branches whipped her and caught on her hair and robe, and blood trickled into her eyes so she could scarcely see. She ignored all that and kept going. She couldn't let Medrhos kill his grandfather, even if it seemed he deserved it – she had to show him!

Fires flashed closer and closer through the trees as ancient pillars loomed above, and angry voices came to her ears. A sword flashed and Samantha never knew afterwards how she managed to slide beneath the blade and drag Karthos out of the way. They both fell to the ground and lay there stunned. Medrhos stood there in absolute confusion within the ring of his men as the torchlights painted their faces with shadow and fire.

"Ancilla!" he exclaimed. His voice sounded sharp with surprise. He grabbed her arm and pulled her to her feet. Samantha could scarcely stand. He hastily lowered her onto a nearby stone.

"What are you doing out here? You're killing yourself!"

Samantha was shaking from exhaustion but she stared evenly into his eyes. "I had to stop you. Medrhos, you can't kill him. He told you the truth when he said he didn't want it done."

"He *lied*, Ancilla," Medrhos growled. "He paid that mercenary to put you in his power. He wanted you to be as a slave!" His hand gripped the hilt of his saber so tightly his arm trembled. "I can't see you like that, I won't see you like that – and the fact that he thinks of you that way is more than I'll ever allow."

"Medrhos, he's retiring tomorrow from your case!" Samantha pleaded. "He's done with you. You're everything he intended you to be and he's done the job that was asked of him. What's the point of punishing him now? He can't hurt you anymore and now he knows better than to try and hurt me. And no real harm came of it, as you can see. I'll be alright soon enough. Please, Medrhos, he's your grandfather, and now. . . he's mine too. You can't satisfy just yourself."

Medrhos' hand shook with the struggle not to let himself go. Karthos stood in silence, awaiting whatever judgement his grandson passed. He was, after all, the Emperor now.

"He doesn't deserve it," he snarled. "To me, his crimes against you are unforgivable. But I do this for your sake, not his." He deactivated the sparking edge of his blade and tore the heavy medallion from Karthos' neck.

"If you continue to work for your precious cult, by this they will know that your work is no longer sanctioned by the Empire, and if you step too far it will cost you your life and their work. Your ship will be ready at dawn. I suggest you be on it." With that, he kicked dirt over the fire, swept Samantha up into his arms, and strode out of the clearing.

~~~

The dawn was chilled and gray with waiting when Samantha and her guardian tiger stood upon the elevated port where Karthos' ship, the *Maelstrom*, was docked. Her engines were running bright with heat, impatient to be off. Still half-dead, Samantha wasn't supposed to be there; Karthos wasn't to have a send-off. He was still inside waiting for clearance. Yet she knew she had to see him leave. At last he exited the hangar, all wrapped in a cloak, papers in hand as he waved his aide to go before him.

"Karthos!"

He halted and looked up. His face seemed older. His eyes were sad yet strangely kind.

"Ancilla. You're ill because of me; I didn't think you'd wish to see me again. But I wished to thank you for what you did last night. I was ready for him to strike but I admit I prefer to live." Samantha gazed at him, hugging herself.

"You aren't the same," she said softly. "I know it. You still bore a crystal within that medallion. But why?"

"It's a long story." Karthos pulled his cloak closer about him and glanced around. He feared that Medrhos would make an appearance and tear Samantha away.

"When the cult chose me to discover the new king, they had to be sure I would not make my own choice, but find the chosen one: chosen by Rätha. That's a dark tale you don't wish to hear. It is the voice I spoke of, and the one you heard, I'm sure, when you were tested by the fire." He sighed.

"Now that my work is done creating the Emperor, the cult has no further need for me to bear the crystal. Had it been otherwise, Medrhos never would have been able to remove the medallion from my neck. Indeed, the thought would never have come to his mind." He hesitated, eyeing the balcony overhead. A figure all in imperial red stood there. Medrhos was watching.

"Listen to me quickly," the old man said urgently in a low voice, grabbing Samantha's shoulder. "Before he comes down here to stop me. Ancilla, once a crystal has been forged to one's will, even when freedom is regained, its effects continue subconsciously. I don't know how I can tell you this, for the cult would destroy me for it. Yes, Medrhos thinks he is immune, but I am sure you will discover that he is not," he said, reading her eyes.

Now it was Samantha's turn to look nervously at the balcony. The crimson figure had vanished. They only had seconds.

"Tell me about the cult. I need to know!"

Karthos shook his head. "I'm afraid you will have to find that out for yourself, Ancilla. I can only guess from certain signs that they do not place their trust in your loyalty, and it was only with great difficulty that I received leave to allow you to become Queen. You must understand that you are Medrhos' partner now and you *must* work with him. One instant of suspicion and you may find yourself dead or in slavery."

A hand dropped heavily on Samantha's shoulder.

"Did I hear something about slavery?" Medrhos asked with a deadly smile. For a second neither Samantha nor Karthos could speak. Silmä gave a rumbling purr and rubbed her whiskers on Medrhos' clenched hand. Then Samantha gave her 'husband' a gentle push.

"Relax, your royal highness, we weren't discussing my imminent suffering," she said, smiling and allowing him to make her lean on his shoulder. "I'm just getting a few pointers on being Queen, that's all."

"Really."

"Of course not. We're actually talking about throwing you into a whale's mouth so we can get a break from you."

Medrhos rolled his eyes but relaxed ever so slightly. He proceeded to lock eyes with Karthos for nearly a minute.

"Your ship is ready and it's past dawn. I suggest you get on it and go, as I ordered you to do."

"As you wish," Karthos murmured.

"Where will you be going?" Samantha inquired.

"Ah, I have one last job to finish," Karthos sighed, "before I find a nice place to retire. Maybe somewhere with beaches. I always liked a good beach. Preferably with no one on it."

"I'm sure I can arrange for that," Medrhos muttered, feeling the blaster at his side.

"I'd like that. Son, there's something I wanted to say to you," Karthos said quietly. "Please listen." Medrhos folded his arms and looked amused but condescendingly patient.

"Proceed."

"I don't expect you to forgive me for what I've done. . . both to you and to your wife. I won't even ask for your favor. But I am sorry that I never had the chance to be a true grandfather to you. I loved your parents and I wish you could understand that I loved you once, before duty called. I know you won't believe that because I wouldn't." He forward and whispered urgently in his grandson's ear before turning away.

Samantha turned to Medrhos to plead with him and saw that he was conflicted. He took the medallion from his pocket and looked at the crystal that glinted through the plating. He threw it to the ground and crushed it beneath his heel. He looked at his grandfather.

"I must admit that without you I'd be nothing; you made me who I am. I wouldn't even have Ancilla. For that reason, may you travel well, Karthos. But for what you've done to my wife I'll never forgive you."

He ordered Samantha to follow him away, taking her arm to support her, and couldn't have cared less when the *Maelstrom* vanished into the thick clouds.

XV

Glacial

Samantha leaned on the ship's railing, her eyes on the crystalline water flowing below. They had sailed deep into the southern seas of Xmara. The sun had set, finding the engineer and Medrhos aboard the graceful vessel in the icy waters.

The 'wedding' was already two weeks in the past. Medrhos had needed to finish a few imperial tasks before they were able to depart, and had also spent that time making sure that Samantha rested and spoiled herself in every possible way. Thanks to his care, she had finally healed from her most recent test, save for the new scar that marred the clean-cut edge of the old one. She lifted her eyes from her own thoughts to view the scenery.

Glaciers like carved diamonds walled in the wide labyrinthine fjords, sheets of icicles falling from them like starlit sapphires suspended mere inches from the water's surface. They glittered with all the colors of the aurora reflected below. The water itself was like the clearest glass. Samantha could see stars shimmering in the depths among the rocks and silverine fish that swam along. It was no wonder that the place had been named *Id-dmurh Tal-estilla*, or the lake of the star's tears.

Samantha felt like a heroine trapped between gilded pages as the reader hesitated to turn to the next cliffhanger; for Medrhos spoke no word as he stood on the bow and the night was still. Karthos had finally lifted his chains from them and judging by Medrhos' silence since, he was weighing the difference between unleashing his full royal powers and heeding the dire warnings which Karthos had spoken to him.

Samantha could only guess that one of those warnings had been to take his advice and move the Marauder ships throughout the galaxy, obtaining a new wave of slaves, lest the cult descend upon Medrhos. She sighed.

She was calmer now that the burden of playing a bride was temporarily lifted, but Medrhos' silence was far worse than his sarcasm. And after he had saved her. . . it was hard not to feel close to him.

"Rhos?" her voice was so soft and her hand so gentle when she touched his arm that it took him a moment to realize she was there. A faint smile crossed his face when he heard that nickname for the first time in over a decade.

"Hm?"

Samantha bumped him gently with her elbow. "I know we're obviously not on our honeymoon, but I didn't call for a statue for company. I know you're stressed, Rhos. As long as I have to play queen, you might as well share it with me."

Medrhos looked out over the fjord. "Sometimes I realize that any young boy who has ever dreamed of an Empire such as mine has no idea what they are dreaming of."

Despite the weariness in his voice, his eyes glinted as he looked up at the sky. Stars and planets whirled above in an iris haze, dancing on through the night. He flung his hand upward. The starlight glimmered on the ruby gems adorning his gloves.

"That is my empire, Ancilla! Stars and planets throughout time, almost numberless, all in servile fear. This is your empire, Ancilla! And now, with you, our empire will stretch even to encompass the Great Galaxy. All will love you as their Queen, and all the ages will belong to you and I." He shook his head with a low laugh.

"Yet these rebels! Mere riffraff, Ancilla, yet they hate me rightly for terrorizing them. But for Karthos I probably would have let you stay my hand, but for now I will laugh at them as a cat laughs at a mouse whose tail is trapped beneath his paw. They think they can upset an empire such as mine. What fools they must be, but I don't blame them for trying."

He shook his head and waxed silent again. Samantha waited patiently, sensing that he had more on his mind. "You heard what Karthos said the night we heard that... laugh," Medrhos said slowly. "Every year at this time we make our biggest raid across the galaxy. This time he wants me to make the decision to expand to the Great Galaxy, and do what I can to take Vestar down. You would be my shield. He has no power over me now and I am loath to accept his advice, yet what better choice could I make?"

His eyes were flashing again. Fearing his train of thought, Samantha shook her head.

"You know, for once I was proud of you, Rhos, when you rebelled against him. Now you think he was right, now that he is no longer able to terrorize you? That came from the Cult, Rhos. It's not something you want to do! Why is it that everyone I love has his Jekyll and Hyde?"

She realized then that she should have modified a word or two, as Medrhos' double-take left him looking more amused than dismayed. Yet, somehow, he simmered down and said nothing about her misstep.

"You were proud of me, Ancilla? Well, how can I take his advice?" He smiled down at her, letting his past fade and his eyes softened again. He looked disarmingly like the young boy she had once known so long ago on Almedra. Medrhos gently took her hands and waited for her to pull away. Samantha sighed and turned her head.

Now she didn't know whether to pull away; she didn't want to. Out here among the stars and waters, he was beginning to feel again like the brother she had loved; was that dangerous? She looked up again to see if he had changed but a sound caught her ears and wrenched every nerve taut.

The creepy cackle rang off the ice surrounding the ship, threatening to crack the frozen walls, and as the ship moved forward the ice formations morphed to resemble that haunted head from Samantha's nightmare. Her nerves snapped and without thinking, she snatched a clump of ice from the frozen railing and hurled it into the supposed face.

The laughing stopped so suddenly that it left Medrhos and Samantha's ears with a deafening ring which threatened to bring on a migraine. Medrhos gently shouldered Samantha behind him as they sailed past the ice that had frightened her. It had lost its face and looked, again, innocent. They tested the silence's length before speaking.

"Medrhos, for once let's work together on something. Tell me what that was."

"I know as little as you. We've both heard it only twice," he replied. He paused and struck the rail with his hands, knocking some of the ice into the water below. Samantha watched the chunks of snow sink in the depths.

For an instant she thought she saw phantoms again as she had on Maedra, but when she blinked, they were gone. She remembered Karthos' mention of the voice of Rätha, whatever it was. But her experience told her that the crystals and the fire basin were possessed.

"Medrhos, you knew when I took the final test that I would hear a voice. There is only one thing *I* know of that it could have been."

"I can think of something," Medrhos muttered, "but my question is why?" He scanned the cliffs. "It threatens you, Samantha. Go inside. I'll try to figure this thing out."

Samantha pulled her cloak closer around her as the air grew colder. Perhaps she should comply. She turned and made her way across the deck.

Without warning, the cliff overhead shattered, spraying the walkway with frozen fragments. Samantha slipped as the weight of the ice swung the ship into a steep list and flung her into the water!

The ice slid with her as the lake water closed over her head and she was sucked down into the ravine below. Thankfully she had the presence of mind to discard the heavy cloak, but even then her limbs could scarcely move in the cold. She gasped as she realized the massive chunk of ice was coming down on top of her!

She never knew afterwards how she managed to get out of the way, as though she had been shoved out of its path. But phantoms seemed to be swimming around her now and she was almost passing out as she struggled towards the surface. Then a hand grabbed her arm and she was pushed upwards.

No, this time it wasn't Marc, but Medrhos. He smiled faintly at the gasping girl as his men threw them a rope and fished them out. The ship pulled clear of the cliffs. Samantha was chilled to the bone. Medrhos stood over her, trying to catch his breath. Someone gave them fur blankets as they cleared the deck of debris so they could get inside. Medrhos suddenly grinned and looked down at his half-drowned queen.

"You'd do well *not* to listen to me *sometimes*, Ancilla."

"I just wanted to see if you'd rescue me," she retorted, teeth chattering. "You'd do well to jump in a little quicker next time. But thank you."

He nodded. One of the men lifted Samantha up and carried her inside; Medrhos hesitated and scanned the now open ocean waters. It had never been known to be dangerous, yet it was distantly possible that the rebels of the Realtra had moved into this lonely territory and staged the accident. Had coming this far south been a good idea?

XVI

Entry

Waking up the next morning was as welcome as the icy bath the night before. Medrhos and thirty of his men – half of those on board – were disembarking the ship in a hydrofoil when Samantha ran out on deck. Medrhos looked annoyed when he caught sight of her amidst directing the men and speaking to the yacht's captain. He was giving orders for the ship to be taken back up the inland lake to Almedran country until his return.

"Stay inside, will you? I don't need you getting sick after last night." Samantha passed up the chance to make a sarcastic reply and demanded his reason for leaving – but only out of curiosity.

"Well, Ancilla," he smirked, "I have a chance to outfox a hunter and I don't think you want to be there to see it."

"Medrhos, no!"

"With luck I'll see you in twenty-four hours."

"Medrhos-"

"Stay inside."

Samantha shut up and fixed her eyes on his face. "Don't hurt anyone," she said at last. "As long as you've forced me to be here, I'll play queen and I'll play it well. My people are most especially those of your domains who do what's right and love what is good; and these 'rebels' are under my protection."

Medrhos raised his eyebrows. "As you wish, my Queen. I shall do what I can. . . which won't be much."

With that he left her and the hydrofoil glided swiftly out of sight, leaving Samantha feeling helpless until she realized that she was free of both Medrhos and Karthos. It took her a few minutes to figure out that this meant she had a chance of escape. But did she want to? And would it be right?

If she left Medrhos she would be abandoning him and his people to their evil ways. But if she stayed, she had eight months to save him, and eight months to be saved, if there was even a chance of that. Marc and Talitha were together – yet both Aiyra and Medrhos needed her. Unless by saving Talitha, Marc had also reversed Aiyra's suffering and the whole family had been reunited.

Samantha tried not to get a headache. She needed to focus. With Medrhos out of the way, perhaps she could raid his office. Gaining access to his computer might mean finding out more about the cult, the crystals, and their true implications for Medrhos. There was only one way to find out. She headed inside.

Sure enough, one of Medrhos' men was guarding the door. She gave him a sweet smile as she passed by on her way to the kitchen, where she requested breakfast to be late, for she was going back to her room to rest. And rest she did – for five minutes before climbing out the window and swinging nimbly onto the narrow handrail of the office balcony.

Most of the balconies and the outside of the ship were rigged with various sensors, both for detecting intruders and picking up weather readings. She had heard Medrhos order the system to be activated after the incident the previous night.

Samantha crouched like a cat on the rail, studying the tile pattern on the floor. Her keen eyes were able to pick out the location of each sensor due to a slight difference in the color of the aluminum tiles. If she were very careful, she could cross to the door without tripping any of the sensors.

However, the door was electronically programmed to recognize only Medrhos' voice. The only way she could bypass the voice recognition would be to thoroughly damage both the speaker and the software. It was nothing that a little saltwater couldn't fix. Thankfully, she wouldn't have to climb down to sea-level to get some.

A puddle was awaiting evaporation in the balcony corner after its rough journey onboard when the ship had rocked so heavily from the crashing ice. Samantha carefully slipped off the railing and picked her way across the balcony.

After unscrewing and removing the panel covering the speaker, she scooped some water up in her hands and splashed it on the wiring. She heard a spluttering crackle. A deft pulling of the two wires she had left undrenched, and the door slid open.

She moved to enter and then stopped to look at the bracelet on her wrist. She realized that she had never turned the signal back on after her escapade two weeks prior. Without knowing why, she felt the need to flip the switch on again.

The office was as she had expected, dark and strict, yet almost luxurious. The desk and mini armory were there, the digi-map was on the wall; but what surprised her was the bookshelf in the corner, laden with old tomes. The city library had been entirely digital, for physical books were, to the Marauders, archaic, much to Samantha's dismay. What was more, no books had been produced in several hundred years, making these books historic at least; but in truth, they were ancient and written in the old Mândrauer tongue.

One tome caught her eye, for it was lying on the edge of the glass-encased shelves. It was steel bound with a heavy clasp and was marked by red gems identical to the ones on the gloves Medrhos now constantly wore.

Fascinated, Samantha lifted the cover. The binding creaked with age. The pages were worn but the severe black lettering still stood out like cut stone. Samantha, of course, couldn't read it, but she did recognize '*kaltarr*,' the word for cult.

Pulse quickening, she picked up the book and crossed to the computer with its massive screen and dozens of gadgets. Of course, it required a password. Samantha powered it on and promptly forced the machine to crash by powering it off during its startup. She clicked the on switch and the computer asked for permission to repair itself before use. Canceling that, she pulled up the deleted statistics. Then began a simple task of locating, copying, pasting, and deleting a few files until the administrator's screen popped up.

One of the tabs kept the history of the set rotation of passwords Medrhos had entered for weekly resets. Samantha was hard-pressed not to laugh. The passwords were all referring to her! That Medrhos really was sweet sometimes. . . .

She shook her head, smiling, and typed in the password, so easy that she should have thought of it. It was, quite simply, 'Ancilla.' Not a particularly secure password, she thought in amusement. But then there were few brazen enough to hack the Emperor's computer.

Instantly the computer came to life – sort-of. In a creepy monotone it inquired what she wanted. First, she ordered it to stop talking and was glad to see that it listened by *not* listening. It turned off its voice recognition. Samantha made a mental note to reset it before she left, and put the book into the auto-scanner.

While it was scanned in, Samantha took the time to search the computer. 'Crystals,' 'cult,' and 'Rätha' came up with no results, but she was able to find some information on the rebels. In fact, Medrhos had a whole file on them, as was to be expected. It detailed the group's history, strikes, movements, the general area of their base recently estimated (some four-hundred square miles), and information on certain individuals who had been identified within the group.

Samantha passed lightly over the actions and movements segment since that was relatively unimportant at the moment. She was surprised to see that, according to the map of guesswork, Medrhos had ordered the yacht to pass straight through the heart of the Realtra's territory. It didn't make sense.

Tal-estilla wasn't even a traditional honeymoon spot – well, not in the last few hundred years, anyway, and certainly not when it was draped in ice. Medrhos was clearly stressed that Samantha was in danger, and he had already suggested that the Realtra might not consider her any friendlier than their Emperor – but why would he knowingly bring her out here?

Confused, she shook her head and kept looking. Her 'husband' was an unpredictable tyrant. If he were still under the influence of the crystal he had worn many years ago, there was no telling what things he might do despite his own inclinations. Not that she was worried about the Realtra.

She glanced at the scanner and saw that seventy percent of the book had been scanned, and it was beginning to be translated. Samantha turned back to the computer after a hasty glance at her watch. She had been in the office for thirty minutes already. She didn't expect Medrhos back for a couple of hours, unless his 'chance' was being taken not too far way. She had asked for breakfast to be served at eight, and it was quarter to seven now. That gave her approximately an hour to skim the book for clues.

As she waited for the scanner to finish its job, she idly opened a folder on individuals within the Realtra. She glanced through the documents on Kadmos and Cajetan. The information was brief and to the point – both were, to all appearances, exiled princes of the southern regions, thrown out of their kingdoms by Medrhos during his Karthos-instigated wrath weeks before.

Hailing from the now-decimated rebel city of Antiqua, Cajetan was young, about twenty-one with dark hair and ember-like eyes. Samantha was reminded of the wise junglecats of Almedra, sad, patient, and brave, with a vicious pent-up fury for the few that were their enemies.

Kadmos, however, was a different story. The pictures in his file were marked by the traditional mask of his kingdom of Talorn, with its flame-like edge that only showed his bright blue eyes. She could tell nothing of his character, for those eyes seemed shrouded as though with trauma. According to the report, Kadmos had been only an assistant in the court before the elderly King Raytarr had passed the crown to him on his deathbed, having no heirs.

Other images of the two princes after their exile showed them in variants of their battle-garb, fur and leather or sleek black suits with light carbon-steel plating that formed a retractable helmet and armor. Despite their best efforts, the two princes had been unable to keep their previously untrained men together and had been fighting a losing battle against Medrhos' forces sent out after them. That, of course, was before Orion.

Her eyes went to the file on the new champion. A smile unconsciously crossed her face as she clicked on the file and began to read through it. Very little was known of Orion, save that he was clearly a charismatic new member of the Realtra. She glanced through the long list of his daring deeds and was surprised to find an image attached. She remembered Karthos mentioning that Orion was uncatchable, and very nearly unphotographable. She brought it up.

It was a somewhat blurry image, clearly from a nighttime security camera. A group of the Realtra had broken into a Southern military outpost and slave camp, stealing supplies and liberating the slaves there. Orion – presumably – was in the center of the picture, standing before the gate he and his men had just thrown open some distance from the camera. He appeared to be looking straight at it as he and his men began taking over the compound. Even in mid-action he stood tall, and despite the blurriness of the image Samantha recognized him.

He was clothed in different garb, but he was the same man who had knelt at her feet seconds before she had been attacked at the banquet. She couldn't see his face here, for it was covered by a hat and cowl of the Kedras region, with the militaristic style cap and warm woolen mask that covered the face, neck, and shoulders. If it were not for the odd three-star symbol emblazoned on his shoulder, Samantha couldn't have been certain that it was the same man. Yet his bearing was the same, and that could not be hidden by any mask.

Why had he been at the banquet? Had he come to scout out the feelings of the new Queen or to see if there was a weakness he could use against Medrhos? Was he merely spying on the great city? All she knew was that his intentions had been good and that he did not see her as an enemy. She exhaled, not having realized how stressed she had been on that point. She checked the scanner again and saw that it had finished.

"Give me your secrets," she muttered, and began to flip digitally through the translation.

XVII

Archaic

The old pages didn't crack from turning, now that Samantha was reading it digitally, but her brain nearly did. The heavy volume was an overview of the history of the Marauders, or the Mândrauers as they were properly called. It was written in the halting, brittle style of the ancient clan, factual to a T. Whoever had written the book wasn't fool enough to complete the puzzle, but she could read in-between the lines.

The introduction opened roughly around 2700 B.C., detailing the humble beginnings of the primitive Mândrauer clan, a ragged group of warrior-hunters who at first fought amongst themselves, then united to fight everybody else. They had a burning spark of anger and a thirst for war that was intrinsic to their nature. Their stubborn rebelliousness challenged them to become the first to build space-worthy ships (preceded by many crashes and many angry internal affairs) and soon the different families were vowing to best each other in colonization.

A few remained behind on Mândra, their untamed homeworld, but the rest voyaged off into the unknown. Sel'lon, the self-appointed leader of the most successful group of voyagers, brought his people to the desert planet of Aliros. It was then populated only by the Utharian tribe, kingly nomads who lived in near silence as they mined the deserts and built their traditions. They had no need to learn how to fight because they had never seen anyone outside of their group, and within it discord was forbidden and life was forced to run like clockwork.

The Mândrauers leapt upon them the moment they landed, determined to take the planet entirely for their own. Making the Utharians their servants was an ideal set-up. To dominate Aliros and build a kingdom there in the desert would put Sel'lon far ahead of the other voyaging Mândrauers. The Utharians could not resist them, but managed to pause the fighting long enough to suggest a treaty.

They offered to design, make, and give fuel to the Mândrauers for their ships, utilizing the energy from the radioactive minerals they mined, and made provisions for the Mândrauers to build their own government. This was in exchange for the Utharians' freedom and a position as counselors to the new government. The Mândrauers could scarcely refuse such an offer and the treaty was made.

A fortress was built high upon the cliffs, and a village made where the Mândrauers could watch their fuel being created as they also improved their ships. Slowly Aliros began to draw the other Mândrauers who had failed at colonizing, and Sel'lon became their true King. He upheld the treaty, however, and accepted advice from those who had allowed him to take the throne. He became staunch allies with their young leader, Iyilos, and gave him his own daughter, Ereth, in marriage. Utharian and Mândrauer tradition mingled until it was scarcely indistinguishable. The warrior-hunters were especially impressed by certain other crystals cultivated by the Utharians; crystals that gave them power, strength, long life, and wisdom.

The Utharians related the ancient legend to their new friends: eons before, only one man was left to live of the tribe of Uthar when a star fell from the sky and his world went up in flames. He cried out in desperation and heard a subtle voice that assured him he would be saved and see many generations of his bloodline, if he served the Voice. The man obeyed, seconds from death, and a sudden dark shadow fell over him, shielding him from the flames as though great wings had covered him.

Moments later the man awakened in a strange place of steam and gemstone caverns. The dark voice was echoing through the chamber, promising him power and those very caverns for his own if the man not only served him, but made all who came after him in his image. The man asked the name of the voice and was told simply that if he did not comply, then when the shadow of Rätha fell again, it would spell eternal death.

And so the man, Ahtar, had lived and found a wife; he lived to be the eldest of his people and saw many generations. He taught them all Rätha's promises and shared with them his secrets, for when he had awakened again and found himself on Aliros, he had found three crystals in his hand: red, white, and yellow, each possessing different properties.

Red was for kings, ultimate power; yellow was for warriors (all men were then), and white was for the women. These seed-like crystals began to reproduce and grow on stone and water, wherever they were placed, until the Utharians' caverns were encrusted by them. When a child reached a certain age – the age of twelve for boys and seven for girls – they were inducted by a ceremony in which they honored Rätha and received a crystal to wear and utilize.

Before long, the Mândrauers were spreading throughout the galaxy, but the Utharians were dying out, as though they had been drained by using their crystals too frequently. Relations between the Mândrauers and the remnants of the Utharians grew strained, kept only for the sake of the fuel and the ruling of Aliros. Yet Utharian and Mândrauer blood had mingled long enough for the promise not to truly fail. But then the time fields were opened, sucking many Mândrauer ships through and they were lost. In time, however, the tenacious Mândrauers learned to control them and took to the slave trade. The galaxy was theirs for the taking! They pillaged, looted, and burned until they had satisfied their desire for those things and settled down in their trade, granting clemency and relative freedom only to those planets and systems which acquiesced to their rule. Andromeda was in chains.

Now with time on their side, the newly-named Marauders had no further need for the Utharians, being able to travel back in time to obtain the fuel once more, and went to war with them again. This time the Utharians barely escaped slavery.

The Princess Aniceda and her few remaining court members were allowed to leave when she gifted all of Aliros, the mine, fuel secrets, and support eternally to them in exchange only for the promise that the Marauders would not cause her death by abandoning the ancient ways.

Bing, bing, bing! Samantha's alarm began to quietly ring, warning her that she only had five minutes left. She shut down the translation program and pulled the book out of the scanner. Now she knew what Medrhos had meant when they had first arrived and he had entreated the shadow of Rätha not to fall. But that was not all she knew now. There was something very strange that she could see between reading the tome and studying the modern Marauders.

Clearly Aniceda and her followers had become the Cult, whether or not the original members still lived. The Marauders were free, letting the Cult play the ancient role of council, but, as Medrhos had said, the Marauders scarcely followed their rules. They were only held to mutual respect and a few ancient formalities and traditions. They hardly even believed in Rätha now that they were strong on their own, but the powers of the crystals could not be utilized without still following tradition and obeying the Cult's rules on approval and initiation.

Yet there was something even stranger about the crystals. According to tradition they granted power, long life, wisdom, skill, and clear judgement, but in Samantha's experience the crystal had given none of these things. Instead it had controlled her! And Medrhos had told her that crystals were used this way now, and as a punishment as well. When had the transition occurred? Were these a fourth type of crystals that had not been not spoken of? Samantha began to wonder.

The ones used for training and for punishment these days were the same as she had worn, faintest violet. There had been mention of the red crystals which Medrhos now wore, those given to kings. These gave ultimate power to the wearer, but this 'power' was not detailed. She had not seen the other types but she supposed that all women and warriors had worn them at one time.

This too was a change, for in ancient times the crystals had been constantly worn. Karthos had mentioned that the crystals were temporary, but their effect continued after their removal. None of it was making sense, unless these crystals were different from the originals.

Frowning, Samantha flipped carefully through the book and found a drawing of the three types of gems. The ruby gems, identical to the ones on the cover, were a deep wine shade with an amber tone when they fractured; the white was iridescent, and the yellow were tinged green. But the ones Medrhos wore had an almost imperceptible violet hue, and the one within Karthos' medallion had been palest lemon with a garnet heart.

What did it mean? It seemed that these crystals were fakes! The crystals had been dangerous from the start with the strange story of Rätha, but now the crystals betrayed their bearers and did not give them the help they supposed it did. Rather, they were controlled without realizing it. It seemed a plausible thing given that Aniceda's people had been nearly disavowed by the Marauders, which would have meant death for the Cult.

Did Medrhos know? Had he studied the book as she had just done? Or would he be blind to it because of his own subjection to the crystal's controlling power? What did the red gems mean for him now? Was he growing even more dangerous and unpredictable? All she knew was that she had to free him as soon as possible, lest she lose Medrhos to the Cult forever!

Samantha hastily glanced at the clock again. She'd have time to try and puzzle things out further later – for now she needed to get going. She forced her brain to stow away the new info and looked at the clock. It was nearly 7:45. She hastily fixed the computer situation and put the book back in its place. With a last check of the room, she stepped out onto the balcony and was greeted by the welcoming committee.

XVIII

Orion

The wind was roaring and whipping up snow when Samantha stumbled, half-blind, into the ice-cave. A snowstorm had sprung up during the long trek due to the temperamental southern seas. The weather had shifted from a balmy forty-six degrees to ten below. Samantha felt frostbitten even through the velvet and fur costume she wore, and she was shivering so much that she could scarcely catch her breath. The fact that Konstan had been at her side the whole time made it worth it.

Konstan pulled off his mask and shook snow out of his hair. His three companions knocked ice off their heavy leather boots. Konstan turned and gently helped Samantha to break the ice droplets off her hair, for when crossing the deep channel, the wind had whipped them all with the icy water that froze quickly even to their skin.

She eyed the blue ice walls, rubbing her gloved hands together to get the blood circulating through her stiffened fingers. She was a little bit numb both with the cold and the shock that the one called Kadmos was her own Konstan, that he was alive!

"Don't worry, sis," Konstan said kindly. "There are some heated caverns further in. We'll get you warm soon."

He put his arm around her and led the way down the sloping, winding cave. These perpetual ice caverns had been bored through the glacier by giant ice worms, which despite the name, were fuzzy and gentle. He promised to introduce her to the one that contentedly permitted the use of his caves and caverns in return for tasty treats (primarily fish and crustaceans with the occasional sweet cake swiped from the nasty Marauders).

But Samantha heard the soothing sound of Konstan's voice more than his words and her eyes could scarcely leave his face. The veil over Kadmos' eyes was thinner now, but there was a gravity and maturity about him that was new to her, and he gently turned aside her automatic questions, knowing she was not in a state to receive his answers.

The smoothened walkway gradually thinned out into bare sea-stone and the air was growing warmer and saltier like the sea air mingled with a sweet smell – Konstan said something about sea roses and they turned the corner into a great branching rock hall where men crisscrossed their way deep into the utilized recesses of the glacier. The ceiling soared high and was lost among chandeliers of ice, great icicles that had hung for a thousand years and never fallen. They were reflected in the great pool from which the Realtra drew fish and sea-sprung herbs.

Great lamps of fire and phosphorescent crystal lit the hall brightly and cast rainbow shadows through the ice. There were scores of men and dozens of passages that curved out of sight at every angle and height. The air was warm and comforting, quickly melting the ice that still clung to the newcomers, yet doing no damage to the ice that had been frozen solid for millenia.

Samantha was led across the massive hall to the widest pathway at the opposite end, passing the doorways that led to the now well-stocked storeroom in the glacier ice. They passed barracks, a mess hall, and everything a fortress should have. The hall opened into a massive chamber with cathedral ceilings and pillars of ice. An icy ramp curved upwards and around a huge column to their left; they could hear distant voices from somewhere above them. Here the morning sunlight came shining through the thick ice walls, refracting a thousand times and casting rainbows across the floor.

"I'm surprised Orion hasn't greeted us as of five minutes ago," Konstan remarked. "Hang on, sis. Orion!" he yelled. "Where in the heavens are you? Are you going to leave Samantha in the cold or are you going to get down here and see her?"

Samantha briefly wondered how Konstan could be so impudent. She heard the voices break off and someone ran towards the balcony.

"Samantha!"

She heard the voice before she saw him.

"Marc!" Her body snapped to attention as her captain appeared at the balcony railing, clothed in the garb of Orion (he nearly fell over the balustrade in his haste). Yes, he was more handsome than she had remembered, so what was new –

Marc's face lit up when he saw her and Samantha was struggling to keep her heart from melting in relief. He was safe! But she found herself longing to see Talitha appear at his side, to know that his own hurts had been healed.

A moment later Marc was sweeping her into his arms.

"Darling Samantha!" he breathed with a smile.

"But Marc, Talitha-?"

He shook his head gently and released her. He grinned at Konstan and looked back at the girl.

"My apologies for the delay, I was caught up doing some business with that charming husband of yours."

Samantha frowned.

"He's not my husband," she grumbled, annoyed that Marc would think so, and she was still confused about Talitha. Marc just laughed.

"I know, a little bird told me. We had a spy in the palace for just long enough to see the wedding. Would you believe, the slave trader you struck at your 'wedding feast' was Konstan?"

"What - Oh, Konstan, I'm so sorry-"

"Forget it, sis," Konstan said in amusement. "I knew you would hit me. Heh, that was a good blow!"

"Wait, what about Estill?"

"She was one of ours," Marc replied. "But we figured she would be safer in Mal'lon than with us. If we were ever captured, we didn't want Estill to be enslaved, and this way she was able to get information to us." He was studying her face very tenderly. "Enough talk though, my darling, you're chilled to the bone. Konstan, let's get her upstairs and get her something to eat. Then we can tell you everything, Sahma."

Together they guided her up the winding ramp and into a spacious sunlit chamber where the ice had been carved out from the inside in glorious patterns, thin enough to offer a view of the outside snowy plains. There was a long table with rough-hewn chairs, only just vacated by Cajetan and a few of his counselors. A sofa was draped with furs farther back, with animal hides and a few Kedras carpets decorating the floor.

From the scattered furs and the snowbells and ice-lilies gathered about (by Konstan, Cajetan, and Marc no less) it was evident that the room had been prepared for her. When it was used by Marc, for it was his council room, there were no carpets or furs. He preferred harsh surroundings to keep him ready for the day he might fight Medrhos.

Marc seated Samantha on the sofa, taking her coat as Konstan poured a tumbler of sea-rose tea and pearl sugar. It both soothed and healed, and tasted how anyone might imagine morning dew to taste in fairyland. Samantha was much better now, but every passing moment seemed to bring her more confusion as her mind became less numbed.

How had Marc found her, why did he come to save her instead of going back to Aiyra who needed him more? Why had he become Orion and what had happened to Talitha? And how had Konstan lived and become Kadmos?

More than that, her eyes were on the clock hanging above the rock-walled fireplace. Medrhos was due back at the yacht any minute! If he discovered her gone, he would track them down relentlessly if it took him a thousand nights, and if he found that Samantha had gone with Konstan of her own volition, there was no telling whether he'd break his promise of pain or if he would merely lock her in her room until their true wedding day. She groaned softly and looked at Marc.

"I have to go back," she pleaded. "Before he finds you!"

Marc shook his head, perched on the arm of the sofa. "There's no need to worry. Your friend won't be in the area for twenty-four hours yet; I saw to that."

"I'll say you did," Konstan muttered laughingly. "Bringing those old ruins down around him! I'll be amazed if he's not wandering through the maze for a week. But then, Medrhos is clever and knows more tricks than the average Marauder."

Noting the worried look in Samantha's eyes, Marc soothed her and promised that Medrhos was in one piece. Konstan brought Samantha a plate laden with thickly sliced bread, buttered with a thick tuna and sea-cucumber sauce ladled over it, paired with sea grapes and a certain rosy-colored seaweed pudding served with tiny honeycakes swiped from the Marauder stores.

"An odd flavor combination, I know." He smiled slightly at his sister's expression. "Trust me, sisia, you need all of it."

Marc went with him to get plates for themselves and then the three moved to the council table. Samantha soon discovered that the odd breakfast was strangely good. She did not want to eat, however, for answers to her questions seemed much more palatable. She agreed to eat only once the two princes had acquiesced to her request.

"We will tell you, but briefly, for there is enough apiece to fill a history book," said Marc, "and I sense you have much to tell us as well."

At Marc's bidding, Konstan told his own tale first. After the blast he had found himself in a strange world, which, to all descriptions, was not too unlike the time tunnel the other two had been in. However, instead of hurtling through time, he had found that the moment he thought of a time and place, it opened before him, only to shut when he thought of something else.

Eventually he took the chance and, resisting the urge to return to his parents, chose to suffer Aiyra's fate and was enslaved at the burning of Cytha. Being out of time, he found he did not grow older as Aiyra did, leading the girl to think that his race possessed lengthened lives. He was a merchant's slave until the day Talitha died and he had run after Aiyra's kidnappers.

Sneaking on board their ship, he soon found himself among the Keltarrs. And, he told Samantha, he had witnessed the implant being given to Aiyra.

"From this I know how to remove it," he said aside, "although reversing its effects was never on the Keltarr agenda. That, the Captain can help with but he'll tell you that later."

He himself had not been found useful as a Keltarr slave so he was sent to the auction block. It was the last time he had seen Aiyra before seven years of memorizing her tears as he silently served the Kedras court and prayed for the day he might see her again. He had lived fourteen years in exile and pain, not aging a day physically but greatly in mind and spirit.

Samantha stared in silence, finally understanding why her dear Konstan was so different and so mature. She noticed him caressing the woven ring on his finger as he stared at the wall with a vague look of pained memory.

While Marc and herself had seen Aiyra within the last six months, Konstan had been separated from the child Aiyra for seven years, and from the Aiyra he loved for fourteen. And the terror of those fourteen years was the change – the terror of not knowing whether the Aiyra he loved was the same, nor whether his love was the same. It was a trial only Marc could fully understand. But memory was bound in that band on his finger -

"She gave you her ring."

Konstan stirred. "Just before I – died – yes."

He looked amused, for he both remembered dying and not dying, two separate memories of the same instant. Now Samantha realized the same, but one memory of an azure flash before the explosion, the other of rose.

"As for Aiyra," Konstan murmured, "nothing can make me happy, not until I see her face without tears." The young prince sighed heavily.

"Aiyra is alone now," Marc said slowly. "My poor baby girl! I wish I could know if she's alright."

Samantha touched his shoulder.

"Truitt, Elise, and Pell will be taking care of her," she comforted him. "I'm sure they have done what they can regarding the implant. Perhaps they have removed it using the plan we had before the attack."

"The fact that the Captain and I combined were led to find out how to heal her leads me to think probably not," Konstan replied. "I just hope we can get back to her soon!" He paused with a dry smile. "The one good thing is I now have some sort of title besides that of mere engineer," he remarked. He looked at Marc.

Samantha studied both blankly.

"She doesn't get it," Konstan said to him.

"I know, I never told her."

"What? I think you should have."

"Told me what?"

"Oh, just that when he married Talitha he became the Prince of the Cythians."

"Wait, you're what?! Oh, that's what Medrhos meant!"

"Now what?"

"He said something or other about the prince of the enemy of his people being taken care of, or something like that."

"If I'm lucky," Konstan smirked, "he might have a second one to deal with."

Samantha choked on her coffee.

"What, I thought coffee was the best thing in the universe?" the young engineer-turned-prince grinned.

"It is, but I just realized, if you marry Aiyra I can't marry Marc, and if I marry him you can't marry Aiyra because you're my brother and she'd be my daughter-"

Now it was Marc's turn to choke.

"I think you just jumped the gun on him," Konstan drawled, highly entertained by the whole conversation. Samantha grouched. Marc was cracking up.

"I was being theoretical," Samantha protested. At least Konstan was smiling now. Marc leaned over and kissed Samantha's hand.

"I'll take that into consideration," he teased, and let it be.

"Technically I'm not your brother, you haven't even officially adopted me," Konstan said calmly. "So I don't see a problem with two engagements."

Samantha flung a piece of her toast at him and relented. "Hurry up and tell me your story," she grumbled to Marc.

He recounted the first test he had undergone, but also told her about his family history.

"To quote Konstan, *technically* I was born in 1381 A.D.," he said wryly, "so you could consider me approximately 1,100 years old if you wanted to."

Samantha felt another headache coming on and dropped her head in her hands, still staring at him.

"Oh, don't worry sis," Konstan gently patted her shoulder. "He isn't really!"

"Oh, definitely not," Marc assured her with a gentle smile. "I'm not nearly that wise so isn't that evidence enough?"

He then told her of finding Aiyra again and noted that while Konstan knew how to remove the implant, he himself knew from Talitha how to heal Aiyra's nervous system, for the herbs Talitha had touched and tended still grew beautifully wild on Maedra.

A chill ran through Samantha at the beauty of this and the threads that God had already woven through time. Marc recounted Talitha's death and it was evident that he was now at peace.

"I'm glad you were able to say goodbye at least," Samantha said softly. "She needed you."

"Yes," Marc murmured. "If God had not let me be with her I think. . . I think as it first played out she might not have had the courage to die without fear, and now Aiyra will no longer suffer from not saying goodbye. I wonder, though, whether she remembers both timelines since you and Konstan both remember his death and yet not."

"I still wonder how," said Samantha. "Who or what saved Konstan? If it was a pure miracle then I think you would only have one memory. It seems that someone, perhaps one of us, has or will change something that saves you, Konstan."

"I think the same," Konstan replied, "and I'm grateful for it whether or not we ever find out how it was done." They allowed Marc to continue his story.

As far as how Marc had become Orion, it had been simple to commandeer a Marauder ship during the commotion of the Aliros revolt, and the work of a mere few hours to learn how to use the time controls. It had quickly brought him to Mal-lon, but in the middle of the terror of the South: a gargantuan blizzard raining knife-like shards of ice and snow so thick and heavy that the ship quickly became overweighted and crashed, leaving Marc to stumble onward with only one thought of getting northwards to Samantha's side. But nothing could have kept him alive in that storm, and it soon had beaten him mercilessly into the snow where he would have been eternally buried if not for Konstan's timely arrival.

Samantha interrupted him to find that indeed, it was that same night she had dreamt of his struggle in the snow. Now she knew why she had been startled awake with the thought of praying for him! For Konstan had had no intention of entering the blizzard, but the life-support generator had ceased to work, necessitating retrieval of emergency supplies: minerals they had learned to use to supply power. Those had been forgotten when he found Marc, but it was alright because a few spare parts from the ship worked well enough.

"Oh, and of course everyone loved having the hero of the battle of Maltara to lead them," Samantha teased. Marc made a face at her and threatened to force-feed her if she didn't finish her breakfast.

"Once you've finished, I think it's your turn to tell us about this-" he added, gently touching the graven scar on her brow.

Samantha obeyed and told them everything that had passed in those long months. She was glad that her audience was composed of good listeners, for even when she spoke of her many ordeals, Karthos, and the crystal, they only moved closer and did not interrupt save with their facial expressions. Instead, she interrupted herself when she saw how strained they were.

"I'm perfectly alright now," she said gently. "I was able to hold my own for the most part, and I'm glad that it did seem to melt Medrhos."

But then she told them of the laughter and the wild tale of the Cult and the crystals. Marc slammed his fist on the table.

"Crystals! Talitha was telling me of them, and how Daruth was only a puppet of the Utharians – Now I know what she meant! She told me if I saved her – I assume I would have been killed, and she said that her will would be forced. . . Daruth had been trying to place the crown on her head, it must have had a crystal in it. . ." he began to pace restlessly, shaking his head, then stopped and looked at her.

"I'm glad you are safe here with us, Samantha. . . you have been up against more than I knew, and he could have killed you just as Daruth killed Talitha – and I would have lost you just as I lost her the first time." He came and drew her close, wrapping his strong arms around her. "I don't want to go through that again," he whispered.

"Samantha," Konstan said slowly, "You think that Medrhos' unpredictable behavior is linked to these crystals, don't you?" When she nodded he voiced something that had been worrying him for years.

"It's a strange thing, but. . . while I suffered with Aiyra it seems almost that there was a plot against her, for they treated her differently and she was purposely moved amongst all the worst slave planets in the Marauder timeline. If Medrhos knew when Talitha died-"

"No, he wouldn't have, not even to punish Marc!" Samantha insisted but there was a great doubt in the back of her mind.

"Relax, sis. . . ." Konstan murmured. "I'm not saying *he* did it."

"The cult," Marc said darkly. "And they could have done it *through* him." Samantha looked so upset they both had to hug her.

"It's alright! Look, it doesn't really matter now, does it? She's safe and you've been keeping Medrhos so busy his slave traders haven't even gone on a single hunt," Konstan pointed out. "So we can safely assume that they haven't tried anything even though they know Marc isn't with her. At least, we hope they haven't."

"You're just making it worse," Samantha murmured, taking a spoonful of pudding and dropping it back on her plate with a sudden lack of appetite. She looked back up at the men.

"If I hadn't experienced all of this, I would have thought it was only the Cult making things up to enforce their rule on the Marauders," she said gravely. "But it could spell death for all of them. Now I know, though you wish me to stay, I can't abandon Medrhos and his people to this. If I can fight it, I know I can lead Medrhos to do the same. He's already inclined to it."

"But you can't predict his actions," Marc countered. "If he's controlled, he could kill you in spite of himself."

"And if I stay here, he'll hunt me down if it takes a thousand nights and you will all be slaves," Samantha reminded him. "And if he finds out that I came with you of my own volition, it will be worse."

"She's right," Konstan admitted. "There's no sense in provoking him now, or we'll all end up like Aiyra, probably worse if that's even possible. That would render us useless in fighting slavery."

Marc exhaled. "Three months at the longest, Samantha, no more. If something happens and you need us, use this." He pulled a small device from his pocket. "It's an invention of Konstan's - it sends a signal on a time-wave, so we'd receive it five hours before you need us. It blends with the radio waves generally utilized by Marauders, reversed, so it is virtually undetectable by their systems." He gave it to her and she slipped it in her pocket.

"Stay with us at least until nightfall," Konstan urged. "The weather will be calmer then, the yacht will be near Almedran-town, and with any luck they won't know you've been away."

Samantha highly doubted the last bit but acquiesced when Konstan told her why – a simple transceiver that mimicked her voice had been linked to the intercom in her stateroom, and was set to inform any callers that she was tired and wished to remain in her room until Medrhos' return.

Of course, if someone became suspicious and forced open the door, she would be found out, but with Medrhos' men it was unlikely. Even if they did suspect they respected her too much to prove themselves right.

Samantha spent the rest of the day in much-needed relief and rest, despite a nagging sense of urgency that chilled her through every now and then, as she followed Marc and Konstan about. She was introduced to the ice worm, as Konstan had promised; the huge, ice-blue 'worm' with its gentle eyes, soft fur, and cute grunts and squeaks was not what Samantha had pictured feeding crunchy honeycakes to.

Mr. Snuggles, as Estill had insisted on calling him, enjoyed the snack very much and quickly decided the newcomer was his favorite. He tried to follow her as she left with the prince, but moaned sorrowfully when he realized there were too many men in the cave. Samantha felt sad and quickly plucked him a large sea-rose as a final tasty treat, which cheered Mr. Snuggles up enough to munch it while they departed.

Samantha had one more necessary introduction – to Prince Cajetan, who had dutifully busied himself with the men, understanding only too well how much private time was needed for the other two princes to be with Samantha. Marc, needing to depart for a study of recent activity at the southern Marauder outposts, left Konstan to guide Samantha to the quiet warrior prince.

With his dark, sorrowful eyes, grave demeanor, and the gentleness with which he took her hand, Cajetan seemed more like the type to be found in a monastery or a palace library than in a war. She soon found out why.

Konstan greeted his friend in a foreign tongue that Samantha could not understand; it was probably a subdivision of the Marauder language, blended with the language of their respective cities. Switching back to the Common Tongue, Konstan introduced Samantha.

"She's the one we told you of," he said. "Medrhos took her from us, but you know her reputation as queen."

Cajetan turned his ember eyes on the young woman and studied her face.

"You are the one who holds her own," he said, with the shadow of a smile. He gently took her hand in greeting, bowing in the manner of his people and bringing her fingers to his brow. "You are brave to sacrifice yourself in returning to him, rather than staying with us. I wish you did not have to bear the strain for us; there is much to be said of you."

"I do what I can," Samantha answered, thanking him. "You are brave as well, your highness, fighting for those whom the Marauders enslave. There is much to be said of you, I'm sure, but I know very little about you."

"What is there to say?" Cajetan replied, turning and strolling with Konstan and Samantha through the pillared halls.

"Much," Konstan smiled, gently punching his friend in the arm. His face turned grave. "She will understand, my friend; *natha lin, allanya to-vin. Valanara crystalli, varke.*"

Cajetan looked again at Samantha, studying her eyes, noting all the Marauder elements of her costume, but the silver Almedran earrings and the Holy Face medal that here, she could wear openly.

"Very well," he said at last. "Please forgive me, *mela Atanya*. While I spoke well of you, I did not trust you, for while being not against us, and protective of the slaves, you have not fought Medrhos as I might have expected. I was afraid he had begun to turn you; but Konstan tells me you resisted it, and well."

"I forgive you," Samantha smiled. "I understand your distrust. Resisting has been difficult, but not futile; it was Medrhos who, after I lasted long enough, was angered by my pain and freed me from it before I could break. If not for him, I surely would have fallen then. He is not a lost cause," she added, softly. "I intend to do all I can to turn him, but I have found that there are darker things at work than I knew, though I should not be surprised."

Seeing the frown that creased Cajetan's brow when she spoke a word of hope for Medrhos, she related all she knew of Rätha and the crystals. Cajetan mulled over her tale for many minutes, as they stood at an icy window and looked out over the snowy plains and distant fjord.

"I believe you," he said at last. His ember eyes sparked briefly with pain and anger. "For I know that only a dark evil can spawn such a world as this one the Marauders have made. And yet I suppose all have had their own small part in it; mere instants where we have not resisted. . . or even many years. You said you know little of me, *Atanya*. I shall tell you, that you may know of my own guilt, and why I fight, despite our many failures."

Fixing his eyes on a distant gleam on the ice, that sparkled and danced with the movement of the sun and cold mist, he told her of his history. Antiqua had been a prosperous but quiet kingdom. . . full of scholars, a city of learning, knowledge, and peace.

Throughout Marauder history, they had done what they could to protect it from falling to the Marauders, keeping a treaty with them, in which they were granted a quiet life in return for a yearly tribute and a promise of no interference. And so Antiqua had continued in its peace, on friendly terms with the Marauders, though they dabbled not in slavery and did not approve of it.

Slowly, little by little, Antiqua began to turn and its culture of wisdom and learning became gradually attuned to the Marauder empire. Shadows darkened the peaceful halls, even though Antiqua's sorrow for the slaves remained strong.

Then, one morning, Cajetan's sister Lyillya departed from Antiqua with an entourage; she was voyaging to the planet Astafar to meet with her future husband, King Arz, one of the few who stood strongly against the movements of the Empire. After a month's time, Lyillya was to be reunited with her brother. But on her return journey,

Cajetan told them, the Great Raid to initiate Medrhos as the new Lord of the Marauder people, swept through the galaxy.

The waves of that torrent broke the voyage lines between every planet, and many ships were captured; including Lyillya's. The initial panic was soothed by the belief that it would be but a moment's work to find Lyillya and straighten everything out, for surely Medrhos hadn't realized who she was. But the Marauder empire was so heavily swayed by the enrichment of the economy through that raid that finding Lyillya became impossible. Medrhos ignored Antiqua's pleas.

By the time Cajetan discovered Lyillya's whereabouts, it was too late. Her 'master' had caused her to fall to her death, while harvesting blossoms from the towering trees of his crystal gardens. The whip marks on Lyillya's body were the final stroke for the young prince. His sister was all he had, and now his eyes were opened to the errors of the slave trade.

Driven by a righteous anger, it did not take him long to discover that Medrhos himself had sent Lyillya to her new life, and veritably to her death. It took far less time for Medrhos to act, and Cajetan and his followers soon found themselves decimated and driven from their home, the treaty forever in ashes.

"I will do all it takes to destroy this empire, and others like it," Cajetan said to Samantha, his wounded eyes telling the tale more eloquently than words. "But, I will not kill Medrhos if I am the one who faces him. I will not do to him what he did to my sister, for no human being deserves it. If all else fails to change him and if others see that such measures are needed, I will not argue. But if you, mela Atanya, see good in him, I have hope that such measures will not be necessary."

Samantha met his ember eyes in silence for a moment, feeling that she could not say the thoughts in her heart, nor say a word that would heal his wounds. Not only was this a tragedy for Cajetan and his people, but it also proved the theory that Medrhos had been moved to crush both Talitha and Aiyra. For here he had destroyed the Princess who merely dared to marry one who stood against the empire. . . .

Cajetan must have read her thoughts and seen her pain, for he touched her shoulder with the faintest smile that signaled comradery.

"'Twas good to meet you, Samantha," he said softly, and pulling on his gloves, he turned and vanished amongst his warriors.

Finally, the sun set and the stars began to come out. Konstan left Marc and Samantha, to see to it that rations, warm blankets, and hot coffee were being prepared for the cold all-night ride. For a while, the only sound was that of the comfortably crackling fire. Samantha was hugging herself, lost in between worried thoughts of Medrhos, Aiyra, the slaves, and the Realtra, and trying to curb her anxiety with prayer.

A moment later Marc was gently taking her hand. Pulling her to her feet, he threw a blanket over her shoulders and led her to a previously unnoticed stairway at the back of the room, half-hidden by the wall. It spiraled upwards through uncut rock up onto the roof of the ice, turreted like an ancient castle.

The weather had subsided and the moon shone above, lighting the glacier like a river of cut glass. Stars streamed across the sky as though to mirror the ice with their light. Marc leaned close to Samantha, his head alongside hers. He pointed out a gleaming star of pale blue rimmed with gold.

"That is Esta," he whispered. "It's the most beloved star of the Cythians. . . a galaxy, in reality, named for an ancient queen, pure and good, who saved her people. Her heart was so great that Cythians speak of their love only by its light, knowing that it ought to be as good and pure as hers." He looked down at her, seeing the star mirrored in the girl's eyes.

"Samantha, by all that is good and beautiful, by a light greater than Esta's, this is my love for you! That I may love you only if it is God's design, that I love you with His Heart, not mine, as He designed and as your beautiful soul deserves." He bent over her then very tenderly.

"I love you, Samantha! If you deem it right, I'll be ever at your side to love you and to guard you." He smiled and added, "You don't need to answer me now; traditionally you can give your answer in two weeks, when Sacra, Esta's King, is beside her."

Samantha breathed an inaudible reply and put herself in his arms. Her scars were glowing on her skin as Marc pressed her close, his face against her dark hair. For a while they said nothing as Samantha thought deeply, feeling at peace there against Marc's heart. But she thought of Medrhos and at last she gave an answer.

"I love you, Marc!" she whispered, still leaning her head on his shoulder. "But I can't answer you now, for I worry that I may still be meant to marry Medrhos. If I leave him now, all of his people will be scandalized, for even if they knew Medrhos and I weren't truly married by our laws, Marc, they would still consider me his wife. It is a great thing for Medrhos not to think as they do, for my sake. . . ."

She hesitated. "And to choose between both of you is not a question of my heart's love, as I once thought, but holy love. I possess it for both of you; but which requires the better part? That I don't know." She turned a worried gaze upon his face and saw that he was not distraught.

"Whatever you choose, I know it will be right," he said softly. "Don't worry about me, Sahma, for I only want you to be happy and God to be pleased."

"But Aiyra needs me," said Samantha, seizing the thought with relief.

"Even she will be alright, Samantha."

Samantha took a deep breath. She smiled up at him. "Then I'll try to answer you in two weeks."

"You two lovebirds had best get a move on," Konstan's voice came from behind them. "I just heard that an angry king found his way out of that maze."

XIX

Contradiction

The lightweight cruiser zipped over the snowy plain. It was almost midnight now, but it would be a few hours yet before Samantha would be back onboard the yacht. Taking the controls, Marc had assured her that they would arrive a few hours ahead of Medrhos, and insisted that she get some sleep.

"But I can't leave you to drive all night!" Samantha protested. "Promise you'll let me take a turn so you can rest too." Marc turned his head and sent her a smile.

"I've done more than this before, Sahma. Don't worry about me."

Samantha gave in and got a little sleep before splitting the rations and coffee with Marc. It would be a long night. At long last Marc could see the lights of the yacht blinking slowly ahead of them. They had cleared the frozen lands and were within a few miles of Almedran-town. He parked the cruiser and gently shook Samantha awake. The ship was moving languidly enough that they scarcely needed to walk quickly for a couple of minutes to reach it.

"The sensors -" said Samantha. Marc showed her the grappling hook pistol he was wearing on his arm.

"This metal, we've found, disrupts most sensory arrays. As long as we only touch the ship's hull within a two-foot radius of the hook, we should be fine."

And, of course, as long as they weren't seen. They climbed up a rocky outcropping a little ahead of the yacht and waited. Samantha pointed out her stateroom window just as Marc's radio beeped. Medrhos was ahead of schedule and would reach the yacht in twenty minutes. Marc grabbed Samantha and watched as the yacht drew abreast of them.

A few men were on the deck above, strolling and enjoying a few last minutes outside before calling it a late night. That didn't bother Marc – choosing his target, he pulled Samantha forwards off the rock face and they plummeted, free-falling silently towards the water – mere seconds before hitting its surface, Marc fired the grapple and they were pulled upwards in a smooth arc with a perfect landing on Samantha's balcony railing. Marc helped her slip over the bars onto the balcony. He hung there for a moment, looking at her.

"Goodnight, my Queen," he murmured. "Three months, remember, and though I pray that you can save him, I fear I may fail you and lose you as I lost Talitha. But call me, darling, and I'll be here in hardly a moment."

He looked so troubled Samantha wished she could forget all else and go back with him. But she knew she couldn't give up, just as he couldn't give in.

"I know I have to save him, Marc," she whispered. "Though I don't know yet what you will have to save me from, I know you won't fail. I trust you." She kissed his brow so tenderly she reminded him very much of Talitha. "Don't be afraid! You'd better go now before Medrhos finds you."

He nodded and swung off the railing. In a moment he was gone. Samantha felt a heavy weight falling on her again but pushed it aside and entered her cabin. Lyona mewed joyfully and leapt off the bed onto Samantha's shoulder to get a kiss. She stayed there as Samantha quickly slipped into a dressing gown and ran her fingers through her hair. Her mental timer clocked the minutes until Medrhos would arrive.

In just a few minutes she heard the hum of the hydrofoil in the distance, the bump as it docked in the yacht's side-bay, and the movement of men on deck. She flicked on the lights by her bed.

Just as she had anticipated, she heard Medrhos' voice in the hall, and her entrance code being keyed in. A light flicked on asking if he could enter and she unlocked the door from her bedside. The door swung open and the Marauder King entered. He stopped short.

His clothes were worn from scrambling about in the underground ruins but he was otherwise unfazed. He did look surprised, however, to find that Samantha was in her room. He motioned for Coran to leave and shut the door behind him. Medrhos turned to Samantha and wasted no words.

"You didn't stay in your room all day, did you. You left the yacht."

Samantha's eyes flickered. What could she say?

"Your mistake was to not fix the mechanism on my balcony door. I won't ask where you went because I already know. I won't ask where their base is because I honestly don't care."

Samantha stared in surprise. If he had known who Orion was, he'd care, but he sincerely wasn't worried about the Realtra's interference or the possibility that Samantha's actions could indicate betrayal? But then, he trusted her.

"As for the computer I can't blame you for doing it; but there are some things you shouldn't know. I wanted to keep you safe from all of it, Samantha."

So then, Medrhos did know these things – had they not registered with him due to the crystal's interference? The girl got up and hugged him gently. Her tensed heart began to beat easier, relieved that Medrhos was neither furious nor revengeful now.

"I'd rather you didn't bear it alone," she said softly, looking up at him. "I love you, Rhos, like the brother you used to be to me."

The King smiled then. "Well, that's something at least. We'll talk about all this in the morning. For now, get some sleep. We'll be staying in Almedran-town for the rest of our trip. Goodnight, my Queen." He bowed laughingly and made his exit.

Samantha stared at the door for a few moments. Medrhos knew, but he didn't know. He didn't care about the rebels, yet he did. He cared about Samantha's actions, and yet he didn't. There was something so safe-feeling about him now, but there was also something very strange that she couldn't label except as a spirit of contradiction in the best scenario.

But it might not even be Medrhos. . . she felt something sinister, and felt that it knew nearly all she knew, and that only by a saving grace were its ever-watching eyes sometimes covered. She knelt to breathe her prayers. Whatever it was, she felt it being held back now so that she could sleep. It could wait until dawn.

XX

Hope

Sunlight streamed across the mountaintops, catching on the dew-strung webs woven across the countryside, catching fire in the droplets and turning them rainbow hues.

Samantha laughed, took her brother's hands and danced around the garden with him. Her mother was laughing as she wove the silken cloth she sold. Her father stopped to watch, Gelert bounding along behind him. Samantha ran and he caught her up in his arms.

Gathering silk in the mountains. . . mountain-diving. . . moonlight parties. . . silk-spinning, her family always there. Hardly a moment alone. How had she lost this? Where were they all now. . . missing her?

"Samantha!" It was the lonely boy on vacation. His dark eyes snapped with excitement. "Take me up the mountain," he insisted.

Shaking her head, Samantha led the way. They scrambled up the rocks. Samantha was an avid climber and the higher up she was the more spider-like were her skills. Medrhos leapt from rock to rock, but she taught him how to climb and how to fall without dying.

Soon they were amongst the gentle mountain spiders, and Samantha gathered a strand of silk here and there, never enough to render a web useless. Medrhos watched in fascination, laughing when he got stuck in a web. Giggling, Samantha freed him and ran. She didn't see the strand of silk crossing the gap between the rocks until it was too late – she tripped over it and slid into the rushing mountain river.

If she had been higher up, she might have been safe. But she knew the bubbling staircase rapidly approaching, that would dash her to her death no matter how well she could fall. Every second was her end and she watched in fear as the plummet came before her, guarded by a rainbow in the spray – a veritable gate to heaven, she had to hope.

And then there was nothing beneath her and a thousand tons of water above her, throwing her to the first stair, so smoothed by the centuries that the water threw her out into the air. She saw below her the second stair which she could not escape.

Two seconds more and – something hit her in the side and now she was falling gently, the breeze carrying her away from the water – then she fell and tumbled onto a rough ledge. Medrhos was bending over her.

A densely woven web was draped over a nearby rock, torn from a cave entrance and forming a perfect parachute. The silken strands Samantha had dropped before her fall were in his hand, twisted into a rope that clung now to the cliff high above them. The boy smirked just a little and gathered her up.

"Nice falling," he teased, glancing into her confused green eyes. "Why don't we go back down now. . . and this time, I'll do the falling." He swung her onto his back and took her down the mountain.

Samantha shook her hair out of its braid and stepped out on the deck of the yacht. It was bright and sunny and her dreams of Almedra were not in vain, for the scene was almost the same as she had remembered – the crystalline webs stretched high in the mountains, catching the light; the calm blue sky floating over the hillsides, mirrored in the cyan of the mountain lakes and rivers. Sweet cottages and farmhouses dotted the landscape, and the white *villasa*, or city that felt like a scaled up village crossed with many chapels, gardens, and low stone walls, glistened in the middle of the valley.

It looked like home. Her home. Only, her family was not there. But these were her people.

She breathed in the scent of the wildflowers and distant bakeries, the sound of birdsong and rippling waters. She missed Almedra. And clearly, so had Medrhos.

She took notice of her 'husband' as he stepped down from the bow of the yacht. The wind was playing with his hair and he seemed more relaxed than she had seen him, more relaxed than any time since the days on Almedra. He smiled at her and motioned her to follow him off the ship.

Samantha's jaw dropped. Two CC speeders were parked at the foot of the gangway. She hadn't seen one since she was ten and she had helped her brother Seraph reconstruct one while they lived on Danya. They had subsequently become expert speedsters until Samantha, age fifteen, had entered the Academy of Engineering and spent the next ten years immersed in schoolwork and the engineering field.

"Want to race?" Medrhos grinned.

"Are you kidding me?" Samantha laughed, and leapt on her beautiful wisteria-tinted speeder. She kicked it into gear and smiled at the nostalgic purring sound it emitted. Medrhos swung onto his own speeder, colored a bright blue, and revved the engine.

"Just avoid shooting me down this time, will you?" Samantha said dryly, inspecting the colorful touchscreen panel in front of her.

"Why would I do that?" Medrhos sounded genuinely puzzled. When Samantha looked at him, she saw that he truly was confused.

"When I tried to escape," she reminded him. He frowned.

"I. . . wouldn't have shot you down, Ancilla."

"But you did."

Medrhos stared for a moment and then at last seemed to recall the incident. He paled a just a trifle. "Well, you didn't get hurt," was all he said.

Samantha was confused. They spent a few moments staring at their consoles as though deciding what setting to put their bikes on.

"Shall we?" Medrhos asked, shaking himself.

"Let's! First one to the villasa dumps the other into the first river we come to," Samantha teased, and promptly left him in the dust.

It was a close race– Samantha was in the lead. She loved the CC speeders for their flexibility, for they could shoot off a hilltop, retract the wheels, and glide for several kilometers, or speed through the rivers, leaving rainbow sprays in their wake.

Samantha laughed at Medrhos as she brought her bike to a halt on the outskirts of the villasa. Medrhos shot past her.

"First to the city, not to the outskirts!" he laughed.

"What!" Samantha sped after him and they were nose to nose as they darted through the alleyway rooftops, before skidding to rest in the city center. Medrhos had won, just barely. He winked at her.

"I'll be looking for the first river we come to, Ancilla," he teased. "But for now, allow me to show you around."

He parked his bike and dismounted, Samantha following suit. A cool breeze blew droplets from the great fountain into their faces.

While it was winter just to the south, Almedran-town was only in late fall, and the autumn leaves were gilded emerald, gold, and peach.

Children played in the streets, men worked in their shops or hung out at the bars for which the Almedran-countryside was famous, and the women were busy tending the flowering bushes, their laundry, or singing as they watched their children. There were silk-weaving shops, dressmakers, carpentry, cafes, quaint libraries, and tall trees hung with festoons of silk and rose-wrapped swings.

The people were all clad in simple Almedran day dress, but Samantha knew from the decorations everywhere that they were preparing for the rose moon festival the following night, and then they would see the concept of Almedran royal peasantry in full. She could hardly believe it.

"It's almost home," she whispered. Medrhos smiled almost tenderly, his gaze wandering around the villasa. Clearly he loved it as much as she did.

"Are you happy?" he asked.

"Happy... I'm happy that you saved my world and let it live, Rhos." She glanced up at him wonderingly. "You should do this more often, big brother." He only smiled and took her arm.

"Come," he invited her. "I'm sure there are many things you wish to do that you haven't done in a long time. But first, I suggest we change into something more fitting."

He promptly led her into a shop, where the smiling woman gave Samantha a dress which Medrhos had ordered several months in advance. He motioned her to go and change in the dressing room.

Samantha held her breath, hardly daring to believe that she wasn't dreaming, as she put on the corseted silk day dress that was so reminiscent of the house dress her mother had often worn. It was made with the rougher, stronger silk of the younger silk spiders; the naturally iridescent silk was dyed an ombre of autumn green that faded into a golden peach, like the leaves that carpeted the ground. The wide triangular shoulders were cut out in long leaf patterns, with detachable sleeves beneath that wrapped her arms to the wrists. The divided skirt, useful for climbing, was paired with a separate wrap skirt for city wear. She looked in the mirror and was glad to finally see the Almedran reflection return.

Samantha ran downstairs and stopped in confusion. Medrhos, too, had donned Almedran garb; a white tunic patterned with a cobalt sun and rippling waves, paired with a matching belt, breeches, and navy suede boots. He looked so relaxed and smiled at her so kindly it hardly made sense.

"I have a feeling we're being paged," Medrhos interrupted her thoughts. He opened the door and they looked out. The city center had filled with men, women and children, waiting patiently for them to exit. Samantha stepped out and the King followed. There was a respectful murmur until Medrhos smiled and waved to them, and the murmur became an affectionate cheer of welcome. The children came running and tackled the King on the steps.

"Do the magic trick!" one of the boys begged.

Medrhos shook his head and tried to turn their attention to Samantha, but a little girl grabbed his arm and hugged it until he gave in. He drew his discarded blaster and aimed it at the pavement, pulling the trigger. A vortex swirled open. To Samantha's shock, the children all jumped in and the portal snapped shut. The parents were shaking their heads and smiling.

"Medrhos, what-"

Medrhos stopped her, chuckling, and gestured as the vortex reopened on the other side of the fountain and the children tumbled out with shrieks of laughter.

"You silly, don't you think that's a bad idea?" Samantha sighed, but couldn't help smiling anyway. Medrhos got to his feet and took her hand.

"If I did, I wouldn't do it. But that's not what they're here for, I think. They want to meet you. Only a few from this city came to our banquet; Karthos only allowed for a certain few from each villasa, and there are a dozen others beyond the mountains." He turned to the crowd.

"This woman is your queen," he told them. "As you have heard, she is one of you. . . I knew her long ago on Almedra. She will be looking after you, as she knows more about your ways than I, and will better know how to help you." He turned and gave Samantha a gentle nudge.

"Now that you don't have Karthos to punish you, my dear, you may go down to them."

Samantha needed no encouragement, and soon stood among the women. She stopped those who tried to kneel and they hugged her instead. Then suddenly everyone was laughing and started drawing Samantha and Medrhos along through the streets.

"Now what?" Samantha asked, bewildered. She was disoriented from suddenly stepping from Marauder turf into her homeland.

"Like I said, you should know better than I," Medrhos snorted as they were led up a hillside to a white gazebo that overlooked the lake on one side, and the city on the other. In the center was a stone-carved well, around which flowers grew.

The women gently placed Samantha in front of it, and Medrhos was asked to stand beside her, which he did. Samantha saw the children running through the meadows gathering wild blossoms and vines of flowers, carrying it to the maidens who began to weave them into chains.

"Oh no," she whispered to Medrhos.

"Oh no what," he murmured back.

"It's the well-wishing ceremony!"

"So?"

"It's for newlyweds," she explained, still whispering. "Medrhos, I wish you hadn't let them think we're married. . . I can't keep this up! It hurts, and it hurts them."

"Samantha, the Cult will kill you if I don't keep you safe. You need to trust me," he hissed. "I know it's not fun deceiving them but for now we have no choice. And you are truly their queen, even if you are not truly my wife yet. They would understand."

There was no more time for discussion, for the maidens started bringing the chains, and laughing, ran around them, weaving the blossoming vines around their shoulders.

Samantha looked as though she had just been doomed. Somehow, this ceremony with her people was a worse trial than some of the things she had been through. It seemed to her that for the sake of healing the deception she would truly have to marry Medrhos, and that thought was going to weigh heavily on her that day, mingled with thoughts of Marc's gentle proposal. What was she going to do? Never mind that now. . . right now she had to survive this.

The maidens stepped back, smiling, and the only sound for several moments was the wind in the trees mingling with the birdsong. Medrhos was looking tenderly at Samantha, her hands in his.

"Hey. . . just trust me," he said softly.

The people were waiting; traditionally the newlyweds would renew their vows for those who weren't at their wedding, and the couple would make a wish for their spouse, followed by wishes made by each attendee. Samantha looked at Medrhos.

"We can't," she whispered.

"Never mind. I'm not Almedran, so you can put the blame on me for not knowing what to do," he grinned. He took her face in his hands.

"I love you, Samantha. There could never have been a better queen than you. . . or a gentler one for your people." He plucked a flower from the vine that bound them.

"May they love you more than they love me, and may I love you as much as you deserve, and follow you in every way I must."

He dropped the blossom into the water, where it floated like an echo. Samantha stared as a rush of relief pounded in her heart. If that wasn't a prayer, what was it? Her fingers trembled as she plucked another purple blossom.

"Rhos, may I see you as you are. . . may those who hurt you change their hearts, may those who need you come to you, and may I help you and your people in every way my God desires."

She was so nervous she was stumbling over her own words now, and was surprised she had managed to even say them. She turned to cast the flower into the well.

She hesitated, looked at him, and added, "And may I love you the way He wishes, and may you love Him in return."

Medrhos was looking at her. He said nothing, only held out his arms and pulled her close. His lips touched the scar on her brow and, worn out, Samantha dropped her pale cheek to rest on his heart.

XXI

Falling

The next morning the sun rose to see Medrhos and Samantha standing at the foot of one of the mountains surrounding the valley, after a long dawntide walk through the fields. Samantha felt better now, and was closely studying the changes in Medrhos' personality while in the valley. He was so carefree, gentle, and happy – but still reckless, she thought, as he let one of the wild mustangs chase him down, just to swing onto its back, grab Samantha, and take them both for a heart-wrenching ride through a gorge.

Finally, Medrhos chose to let the stallion go, and ditched himself with a neat landing on a rocky staircase carved into the canyon wall. Samantha, left to her own devices, whipped out a length of strong silk, a must-have item for every Almedran, and used it to swing herself off the horse's back and onto the limb of a fallen tree that jutted out over the gorge. She perched there, eyeing Medrhos as she coiled the silk and put it back in the pouch at her waist.

The silk strand was approximately seventy feet long and, being silk from a young spider, was strong yet pliable enough to be untwisted up to a length of a hundred and forty feet. She had missed the freedom that single strand of silk gave her – as a child she had learned to weave it into a weapon, a net, glider, or a myriad of other items in seconds.

"Are you going to come down?" Medrhos grinned.

"Down? I thought we were going up!" Samantha replied, and flipped backwards. The mountain they had abandoned stood nearby; with an inhuman leap, she flung herself to the first mountain ledge. She laughed down at Medrhos who was staring.

"You coming?"

"Since when can you-"

"Jump twenty feet?" Samantha whipped out her silk lasso again. "I'm surprised you didn't know that Almedrans can do that! Do try to keep up, silly boy!"

She vaulted up the rock wall, leaving Medrhos shaking his head before finding his own way up. He might not have had the jumping skills, but he hadn't forgotten the climbing lessons Samantha had given him. He was nearly able to keep up, and Samantha couldn't help but be impressed by her protégé.

Within the hour, they had reached the mountain roof, where the stone leveled out among caves and overhangs. Murmuring brooks splashed all around the pair, sending rainbow spray into their faces. Lone strands of silk were hung everywhere, catching the light with a thousand colors.

Hearing the soft buzz of a distant waterfall, Samantha waved for Medrhos to follow her and they darted through the rocks until they came upon a wide space, surrounded by mountain walls.

A stream flowed over them, falling into a deep green pool below. Here spiderwebs of many designs were strung up everywhere. Samantha looked around. It seemed the spiders were all sleeping in their caves, for they rarely used their silk as a home.

"How many were you able to save?" she breathed. Medrhos ran his fingers through his hair.

"Only a few," he whispered. "We had to breed them, and genetically engineer a number of them to make things work for your people."

"Genetically engineered – seriously? Medrhos, that's dangerous! I mean-" Samantha shook her head. "Thank you. It was good of you to look after them this way, even if it is dangerous." She glanced up at him.

"Ah, well, we have been keeping an eye on the engineered ones," Medrhos coughed. "But they seem to have worked well. Hush, look! There's one now. You can tell the genetically modified ones apart from the true breed by their darker coloring and the patches on their backs."

Samantha looked and saw several spiders emerging from their siestas. Why did it feel like coming home again to see them - she found herself smiling, for these were the biggest, gentlest, and most beautiful spiders any mortal had ever seen.

Their bodies were like iridescent, opaque crystal, the legs long and delicate, their abdomens painted with streaks of turquoise and peach, but sequined with silver mirror-like patches. These mirrors aided the shy creatures in protecting themselves from potential predators, using their knack for illusion to become nearly invisible in their surroundings, particularly in bodies of water.

Medrhos was right, however, one of the three spiders was larger and darker in color, with a smoky gray tint and red and blue stripes instead. The mirror patches were dark brown to match the stones.

"Are their temperaments the same?" Samantha whispered.

"Er. . . not quite. Ours are a little more aggressive."

"Naturally."

Marauder spiders. It could have been worse, she thought. She carefully stepped out from behind the rocks and waited until the shy spiders noticed her presence before climbing down to them.

One of the white Almedran spiders advanced to study her, touching her hands gently with its feelers until it was assured that she was Almedran, too. It also investigated Medrhos, who stood still and let it test the gloves on his hands, as it prodding the gems in curiosity. Then this spider left, content with the visitors' presence.

The huge Marauder spider, however, had stayed still on the other side of the pool, watching with its eight dark eyes. Now that the Almedran spider had retreated, it advanced, pincers clacking. Samantha heard a rattling hiss and realized it was preparing to pounce, thinking that she was a threat. Medrhos stepped in front of her.

"Hey!" he said sharply. The spider stopped, looking vaguely annoyed, but cocked its head towards him.

"The lady is a friend. She's *Almedran*. Don't just attack people you don't know; that's not what you do," the King reprimanded him.

The spider huffed but obediently leaned forward and lightly pinched Medrhos' right hand before withdrawing to watch with winking eyes.

"Yes, I'd say they're a tad more aggressive. Just a tad."

"Sorry about that," Medrhos apologized. He was looking over Samantha's shoulder at a baby spider that had climbed up a rock and was now inquisitively reaching out to touch Samantha's hair.

"Hey," she laughed, and gave the puppy-sized spider her hand. It wrapped its eight legs around it the way a house cat clings with its paws when playfighting, and Samantha lifted it down from the rock and took a seat. The spider promptly undertook its favorite game, trying to catch her hand with webbing.

Unlike most spiders, Almedran spiders spun their webs from their front legs, so the infant kept shooting webbing at Samantha's hand, trying to wrap it as though it were a fly. Samantha only smiled and kept tugging on her hand to make it more difficult. It was much like how Gelert would play with her slippers. In the end, Samantha came away from the play fight with thirty yards of the soft baby silk. She wrapped it into a yarn-like ball and stowed it in the pouch at her waist.

"I think we have a rose moon celebration we need to prepare for," she noted. "Shall we go for a nice fall?"

Medrhos smiled and bowed. "After you, Ancilla. Just don't make me catch you." He winked and leapt from the promontory.

"I'll take that as a challenge, I guess," Samantha grinned, and followed.

Who needed parachutes and ropes, when they could fall and use each rocky landing as a steppingstone or vaulting point, and each mountain stream a slide? The wind helped bear them up and the stones were covered with a thick, springy moss that cushioned each landing.

Samantha reveled in the free-fall. She could see the cornflower blue sky above, with its wispy crown of clouds, the patchwork of the fields and rivers below, and the shining villasa in the distance.

What she didn't see was the dark spider following her, swiftly scrambling down the cliffs. Samantha swung herself off of a ledge and aimed for the one below, reminded of the obstacle course back in Mal'lon. She'd have to take it up as a pastime. She didn't notice the half-formed, slippery webbing that suddenly coated the rocks just as she landed on them.

Samantha lost her footing and her trajectory in the same instant and found herself falling head first towards a sharp spire of rock rather than the boulder she had been aiming for. She tried to twist midair to change the direction of her fall, but she was falling too quickly – she had already passed Medrhos, who had been a ways below her.

She heard him shout and didn't know that he saw the hulking shape of the spider somehow already waiting for her to fall into its trap. Samantha tore the silk from her belt and let go of one end, hoping that it would catch on something. There was no time for a glider, nor even room – she'd have been caught on the rocks and falling again.

Another second and she'd be caught in the spider's pincers, but she still hadn't seen it. It might stop her fall, but no one could trust it not to eat her. Then the silk snapped taut!

Samantha's body snapped with it and she winced. The silk had snagged just momentarily on a branch of mountain pine, but it wouldn't hold for long – Samantha heard the clicking of the spider's pincers and glanced down to see it climbing up, nearly within reach. She had just one chance and only a moment to take it –

The girl kicked off of the wall and swung herself perpendicular to it. She arced out over the valley, clearing the pinnacles, but also negating any chance of finding a ledge to land on. But at least the spider's jaws snapped the silk in half, and not her body!

There was a violent flash of scarlet and a sound like a hundred hissing snakes but the girl was too busy looking for a way out of her situation to find out what her 'husband' had done.

The wind whistled in Samantha's ears as she fell. If she had another piece of silk she could have woven a parachute in time before falling several thousand feet to the valley floor. The baby silk would never hold her weight! Medrhos was now her only chance, but he couldn't save her now, could he?

She turned her head from picking out the site of her crash landing but something hit her in the side, carrying her parallel to the mountain behind her, and down, down to a safe landing on the emerald heights of the foothills. Samantha tumbled onto the grass, surprised to find that she was shaking violently. She brushed her hair out of her face and found a pair of hazel eyes laughing at her.

"Nice fall, Ancilla," Medrhos whispered with a grin as he picked her up.

"How did you-"

"Like I said, I have the power to save or to destroy whatever I wish."

He jerked his head at the smoldering spider mass that hit the ground in the distance and the length of wire which he had created and that now draped loosely on the ground.

"I'm not limited to using spider silk to catch you, my dear. Next time. . . let me do the falling, please."

"Oh, Rhos. . ." Samantha laughed a little and let her head fall on his shoulder. She had a bad feeling about him using his powers again. At the same time, she was relieved that the spider was dead. It was far too aggressive to risk it attacking anyone else.

"You're a good big brother," Samantha whispered. Medrhos smiled to himself as he started down the hill.

"Only the best for you, Ancilla. Besides, I couldn't have you disappearing into a spider's stomach when we have a celebration to attend now, could I?"

~~~

The crickets were chirping a sweet serenade as the stars sparkled over the mountains. The sun had just set and the horizon was painted a bright turquoise, the sky above a deep velvety violet. The Almedrans were all gathered on the banks of the lake, waiting for the rising of the rose moon. Per their connection to the moons of the galaxy via their moon scars, each moon was celebrated as a work of God's art, and in thanksgiving for the special gift noted during that season.

Hence, the rose moon for the month of Almedran roses; for the rainbow shades of the healing blossoms, rescued from the planet like the spiders, had been found under every rock, on every mountainside, and in every garden. The flowers were held precious for their healing powers, and were heavily relied upon for culinary, crafting, and everyday home uses.

Samantha and Medrhos were standing together, watching for the first sliver of the pink moon to appear; unlike moon phases elsewhere, it seemed that nature liked to mirror the names given her by the Almedrans, and often softened its appearance to match.

Slowly, slowly a glimmer of white and silver peeked over the mountain's edge – and then rose more and more quickly to reveal the softly blush tinted moon. Its light brightened the valley, gilding the moon scars on each man, woman, and child, and swung the celebration on.

Fairy lights lit the trees, and lanterns were hung from every bough; candles were set on the lake and every fountain, floating along with the sweet music that began to play. Flutes harmonized with harps, guitars, and unique Almedran instruments of exquisite sound and design. Children frolicked, couples danced, and parents played merry games in the rose-gold lighting. The scent of rose blossoms sweetened the air as Medrhos stood close to Samantha, gazing at the silver scars as she watched her people.

Old memories played in her head. If she forgot Medrhos for a moment, her mind could no longer tell that she was on Mal'lon, for all was the same as home. Yet her heart began to ache. She thought of her family back on Danya: her mother and father, her brother Seraph. She had cut off communication with them shortly after leaving home.

She had told them why, for they knew the story of Medrhos, but nothing they said had ever made her feel safe for them. She hadn't wanted Medrhos to be of the impression that her family would be in her way. . . but now it had been several years since she had accepted or sent any messages to her family, except for a noncommittal update on whether she was alright. It wounded her now, for she realized again how much it hurt them. But she knew she had been right; Medrhos would have deemed them in his way.

Medrhos interrupted her thoughts, plucking a floating rose blossom out of the fountain and tucking it into her hair.

"What is it, my Rose," he said with a smile. He gently touched the beaded sleeve of her gown, so much like the one she had worn the night she had danced with Marc on Maedra. This time the overskirt was scattered with silk roses and gleaming beads of crystal and rose quartz. A silver band around her throat was hung with an iridescent moonlike disk, from which silk ribbons draped around her shoulders.

Oh, so many more memories that brought painful struggles between the love for each – she turned to look at Medrhos.

"Nothing," she assured him. But was it nothing? He was so different here, so wholesome and kind. What if he could talk to Marc – but no, she couldn't risk Marc's identity, for surely Medrhos would change once they left.

"Nothing, Samantha?"

He was even calling her Samantha again? No, she couldn't speak of it.

Keep your mind on the moment, she told herself, and reassured Medrhos that they were only memories.

"Good ones, I hope," he replied. "I think we should make more good memories for you, Samantha. Why don't we start with food? After saving you twice this morning-"

"Twice?"

"Once from a spider and once from falling. They just happened to be at the same time."

"I count that as once, but alright," Samantha laughed, and let him take her arm and steer her to the nearest table, garlanded with ivy and scattered with pink and yellow flower petals.

As they stepped out of the direct moonlight, Samantha's scars flickered and faded again. Medrhos studied her a moment and then turned his attention to the table. Rose mead, berry-blossom ice, and moon milk were the favored drinks; Medrhos took the mead over ice but Samantha took the moon milk, a slightly bubbly, sweet drink with a tropical taste. There was a variant with almonds, honey, and roses, which she tried next.

There were sweet corn and oat cakes with pearl sugar and wildflower icing, stewed blackberry chicken, buckwheat buns, white squash and pumpkin seed soup, potato fritters, and baskets piled high with the latest crop of grapes, carrots, sweet beans, pudding fruit, and soft-skinned lemelons that tasted like lemon curd.

Of course, a rose moon couldn't be celebrated without dozens of dishes made with the rose harvest. Candied roses spilled amongst gem-like pomegranate and rosehip tarts, rosehip jelly with mountain cream, urns of rosewine and lemon rose-water, deep dishes of baked tomatoes and roses, rose-rice, rosehip, strawberry, and cheese salad, and too many things for Medrhos and Samantha to even have a taste of.

Samantha hadn't had many of these things even on Danya, for some recipes had been lost, particularly due to the lack of customary ingredients only found on Almedra. She loved it, but there was still a cold chill deep inside; she was worried about the Realtra, about Aiyra, about her family, and most of all, conscious of the fact that this current peace was only temporary. Soon she would again have to fight to survive in Mal-lon, to fight to save Medrhos, the slaves, and Aiyra. She took a deep breath and closed her eyes.

Now, at least, she knew what healed him. Almedran-Town was so safe, so nestled within the protective aura, so to speak, of the dozens and dozens of chapels the valley held, that even though Medrhos didn't quite care, it still protected him from the influence of the Cult. She would just have to find a way to replicate this in Mal-lon; and for now, she would have to take the chance of his clear mind to speak to him of slavery, and of God.

She felt the chill slipping away, and opened her eyes and ears again to the joyful dance being played in front of her. Medrhos was watching her, for the scars that fascinated him were glowing again on her face and hands.

"You've never seen them before?" Samantha asked with sudden gaiety. "I suppose I only saw you in the daytime back on Almedra, and I had no reason for the scars to be seen in Mal-lon."

"Some would call them truly scars, but I think they are beautiful." Medrhos seemed strangely shy, and he paused before pulling her into the courtyard that was generally assumed to be the dancefloor. He swung her around until they were both dizzy, and the stars were spinning too fast above them and they couldn't tell them from the lantern lights.

Laughing breathlessly, they stumbled to a low rock wall under the trees that guarded the river entrance to the lake, and sat down to watch the dancers and the children play. Samantha's eyes wandered between them and her companion.

The moonlight was shining on his dark hair, highlighting it with silver. Instead of the harsh warrior king demeanor and dress, the gentle nature she was growing used to was there instead, and Almedran garb made it seem as though he could never have been cruel, never been a liar or owner of an empire of slavery. But he was just that, just not here, not now. She had to take advantage of these moments.

Father, help me to help him. Let me be Your hands, Your voice, Your love, Your strength, Your healing, Your safety, for him, if he cannot come straight to You.

She leaned over and touched his arm. He glanced at her in surprise as he always did. This time, however, there was no arrogance to follow, but only a very sweet glance and he covered her hand with his own.

"Yes, my Rose."

Samantha smiled a little. "I must be the thorny kind, Rhos."

"Yes, but it only guards the fact that its sweeter than the other roses," he replied, eyes smiling. "What is it, Samantha?"

The girl admitted that there was much on her mind, but there seemed to be too little time.

"Too little?" Medrhos smiled. "I can make time, if you really need it."

Samantha laughed and assured him it would be alright and that there was always enough time for what was necessary.

"I just need to find out what *is*," she murmured. Her eyes wandered the fairytale of a garden. "Sometimes it is very hard to know what to put first, and what last."

"Mm, I know what you mean, Sahma. I try my hand at it every day but I'm not sure I've ever succeeded in learning how it's done."

He paused and waved to Coran, who had appeared in the midst of the celebration and was looking for him. The King's aide approached with a quiet apology to Samantha before turning to Medrhos.

"It is done, my lord. We got all of them."

"You checked for all the tracking signals?"

Coran nodded and Medrhos clapped him on the shoulder. "Good work, to you and the others. Tell them to enjoy the feast."

"Very good, sire," Coran smiled, and bowing to them, left.

"What was that about?" Samantha inquired, realizing that her hand was on her heart. It couldn't be the Realtra –

"I sent them out to kill our spiders," Medrhos replied. "After one attacked you, I didn't trust the rest. It poses no danger of any kind to your people now; by this time there are plenty of Almedran spiders without our own. I only hope that their personality won't have been changed by breeding. I think it will be fine, but we'll keep an eye on them."

Samantha gave him the hand that she had taken away when Coran had stepped in.

"Oh Rhos, I don't understand. Sometimes, like now, you're wonderful, and I love you. Thank you for destroying those spiders, Rhos – this is truly you, when you protect my people and I, when you give us a home. This is what your people should be, and are; but instead, with others you take them from their homes, take them from their families, take them from their lives, and even *take* lives. You spend your life destroying, not saving, but can't you see that this is your calling? Here, you seem so free and in your own mind. You love, but you don't hate. You're gentle, not vengeful. And this is what I wished to speak to you of. . . I have to know, while you are here and before this time is gone, who are you, Rhos? Do you truly love slavery, and hate Vestar and the Order? Do you really wish to destroy the Realtra?"

Medrhos seemed perturbed, as though he were searching for an answer that didn't sound like a lie to please her.

"Sahma. . . remember how you reminded me of your attempted escape, and how I forced you to crash? But I didn't remember? Samantha, here, I remember only vaguely what my life is like, until you remind me of it. Here, I have no interest in slaves, or Vestar, or the Order, and no desire to go after the Realtra. Yet. . . I know how I am elsewhere. Your valley here has peace, Samantha, that my anger must retire under, but I can still feel it. I know it won't stay quiet once we leave." He turned his head away.

"Promise me one thing, if you can, Samantha. Promise me that you won't despise me after all we've done here." He turned pleading eyes to her face. "You promised you would love me as much as you're meant to. I can tell that you love me, Samantha, and I love you so! No matter what I do, understand that I would never, ever, purposely do anything to harm you or anyone you love."

Samantha didn't know what to say. What could she say? She couldn't despise him; God wouldn't let her. She had indeed promised, and she did indeed love him, though perhaps not in the way he hoped. Or did she even know?

Why did she have to be one of those girls who couldn't decide? Why did she have to be trapped between two men? Why didn't God just tell her which one needed her love more? But right now, Medrhos needed more help and love, at least sisterly love, more than Marc did.

"Medrhos, I couldn't hate you if I tried," she said gently. "I promise that I won't. God wouldn't want me to."

She paused. How best to ask him how he felt about God? Straightforwardly, perhaps. Medrhos stopped her and arose.

"Even I am bound to powers darker than my own devices, Samantha," he said quietly, staring out into the night. "My people have been bound too closely to them for me to escape as I once hoped."

Samantha said nothing.

"I assume that you now know of what I speak. I know you used the translator on my computer."

Samantha only nodded.

"Then you know why I cannot do as you would wish. But I promise, for the sake of your love, I won't hurt those whom you love if it be in my hands. Samantha, when we leave here, this conversation will never be in my mind again." He looked at her gravely.

"I understand," Samantha murmured, and turned away. They remained there listening to the music, the lake waves, the gaiety of the Almedrans, and the soft chirping of birds and crickets.

"Come," Medrhos shook himself and lifted her to her feet. "Let's walk, my Rose, and enjoy the peace we have now." He put his arm around her and they walked along the low stone wall until it crumbled to an end. They found themselves among the daisies on the river bank. Medrhos paused.

"There is one thing I have forgotten," he said abruptly.

"What is it," Samantha sighed softly, too dimmed by her failure to notice his laughing eyes.

"I forgot that I won the race." He grabbed her around the waist and swung her over the banks. She went in with a splash!

Laughing, Medrhos crouched on a flat stone as Samantha surfaced, gasping.

"What a surprise that this was the first river we came to; couldn't miss my chance, now, could I?" he teased.

"You-you-" Samantha spluttered, but now she was laughing too. Her hair was falling in her eyes, her dress drenched, her scars glowing – she was a sight. She accepted the hand that Medrhos offered her and waded up to the bank. She leaned her arms on the rock, still holding his hand.

"I wasn't planning on going for a swim," she remarked. "But hey, the water's nice, so why don't you get in?" She yanked him off balance and he tumbled over her shoulder with a splash.

"What, you-" Medrhos sent a wave at her and she deflected it, splashing him back. The battle would have continued if Coran hadn't suddenly appeared on the bank. He looked torn between laughter at the sight and anxiety over his message.

"Sire!" He gave Medrhos a hand, and then the King lifted Samantha out and let her lean on him.

"What is it?"

"It's bad."

Medrhos braced himself and the laughter went out of his eyes. "How bad?"

"Interrogator-level bad," Coran murmured. "They'll be here in a week."

Instantly Medrhos changed. "Tell the men we're leaving as soon as the feast is over. Samantha, come back with me to the ship." He looked into her eyes.

"I won't forget my promise. Don't forget yours. . . I fear it may be a hard one to keep." He grasped her arm, threw his discarded cloak over her shoulders, and took her away through the trees.

www.ingramcontent.com/pod-product-compliance
Lightning Source LLC
Chambersburg PA
CBHW010806250626
47156CB00010B/3013